the distance to home

the
distance
to home

Jenn Bishop

Alfred A. Knopf New York

THIS IS A BORZOI BOOK PUBLISHED BY ALFRED A. KNOPF

Visit us on the Web! randomhousekids.com

Educators and librarians, for a variety of teaching tools, visit us at RHTeachersLibrarians.com

Library of Congress Cataloging-in-Publication Data
Names: Bishop, Jenn.
Title: The distance to home / Jenn Bishop.
Description: First edition. | New York : Alfred A. Knopf, [2016] | Summary: Baseball player and superfan Quinnen must struggle to deal with her older sister's death in a story that unfolds between two summers.
Identifiers: LCCN 2015018540 | ISBN 978-1-101-93871-3 (trade) | ISBN 978-1-101-93872-0 (lib. bdg.) | ISBN 978-1-101-93873-7 (ebook)
Subjects: | CYAC: Baseball—Fiction. | Sisters—Fiction. | Grief—Fiction.
Classification: LCC PZ7.1.B55 Di 2016 | DDC [Fic]—dc23
LC record available at http://lccn.loc.gov/2015018540

The text of this book is set in 12-point Berling.

Printed in the United States of America
June 2016
10 9 8 7 6 5 4 3 2 1

First Edition

For my parents, Colin, and Bryan.
And for Nisha, because I promised.

1

{this summer}

I used to think if you got woken up in the middle of the night, you needed to watch out. In movies and books, bad things only happen in the middle of the night.

But it's not true. Something bad can happen in the middle of a perfectly sunny day.

When Dad starts up the truck, the red numbers on the dashboard clock surprise me. It's nearly 2:00 a.m. He hums to himself, lost in his own world. He didn't used to be like this. Sometimes it seems like Dad from last summer and Dad from this summer are two totally different people.

Dad from this summer doesn't tell me where we're going or why he told me ten minutes ago to get dressed and meet him outside. Only that it was a good surprise. Whatever that means. It's been a long time since we got a good surprise.

After a few minutes of quiet, Dad turns on the radio. In the middle of the night out here, there's never much on except for *After Midnight*, this show where people call in to dedicate songs to people they loved until something went wrong.

"Our caller tonight is Abby," the DJ says. "Tell us your story."

"Sure. Two years ago, I met the love of my life in line at the grocery store. How cheesy is that? I know, right? We spent every waking moment together, and six months later he proposed. We were supposed to get married this weekend, but Trevor had a heart attack when he was running a marathon two months ago."

Dad reaches his hand out to turn the radio off. "Don't," I whisper. He puts his hand back on the steering wheel and sighs.

"He didn't make it," Abby says. "I miss him so much. I think about him all the time. Can you play Bette Midler's 'The Wind Beneath My Wings' in honor of him?"

"Going out to Trevor, wherever you are, from Abby," the DJ says, and the song starts to play.

I found the radio show one night when I couldn't sleep. Dad and Mom don't know that I plug my head-

2

phones into the old stereo in my room and listen after they go to bed. It helps, hearing other people's stories.

"The song won't bring him back," Dad mutters under his breath.

It's not supposed to, I want to tell him. That's not the point. But we never talk about this stuff anymore. It feels like Mom and Dad think I'm done talking about it, after my appointments with Miss Ella and her cracked orange leather chair and that plant she always forgot to water. But I wasn't ready then. I barely got started.

I tap my fingers on the side of the door along with the song. "Where are we going?" My voice is shaky, like I haven't used it in a while. Which I guess is true. There's no one around to talk to anymore after Mom and Dad go to bed.

"The Millers'. We're getting a boy this summer."

"A boy?"

Dad doesn't answer me at first.

"What do you mean?"

"The players got in late tonight. They flew into O'Hare, and Jim—I mean, Mr. Miller—just got back with them. We're going to host one this summer."

"We're getting a baseball player?"

"Yup." Dad raises his eyebrows in that mischievous way he always used to, and for a second it's as if Dad from last summer is back.

Our town is the home of the Tri-City Bandits, a

minor league baseball team. The players don't make much money here, and won't until they reach the big leagues, so for the summer they stay in people's houses for free. Mostly retired people who have extra bedrooms, but sometimes people who still have kids at home.

"One of the Bandits is going to stay in *our* house?" My voice gets higher with each word. I can't help it. My sister, Haley, and I always wanted one of the players to stay with us. Every summer, Haley would beg Mom and Dad, but they always said no. They were too busy.

"Mom knows?" I ask.

Dad clears his throat. "Your mother and I thought this would be a good thing for us. And for you." He glances over at me, like he's waiting for me to agree.

Maybe if there's someone else around the house, Mom will have someone else to hover over. Busy Bee Mom, Haley called her. She'd joke about how Mom would knock on her door five million times every night with questions about school and Haley's friends and then buzz her way over to my door to check in on me and my homework. Back and forth, back and forth. I could picture Mom like that at the community college, too, where she used to teach English. Buzzing from one desk to the next.

Now she has no one else to buzz to. Only me.

But not anymore. Not this summer, anyway. Me and a baseball player.

4

I stare out the window at all the cornfields, but it's more like I'm playing a movie in my head. I can see it already. There's a super-tan guy living in our house for the whole summer, taking me and my neighbor Casey out for ice cream after the games. We can sit in the seats right behind home plate and shout out our player's name. And he won't just be a name off the roster, some guy who signed a foul ball I happened to catch. He'll be my friend.

I want to tell Haley all about it. To have her sitting in the spot next to me, the spot in the truck that was hers.

I blink my eyes real fast so tears don't have a chance to form. We pull into the Millers' driveway, and Dad puts the truck into park. I dig under the seat for my glove. It's got to be in here somewhere.

"You coming, Quinnen?" Dad is already at the Millers' front door.

"I'll be right there!" My fingertips touch the worn leather. I reach my arm in deeper, until I have a good grasp on it.

When I pull the glove out, it has dust all over it from being in Dad's truck so long. I slide my hand in, but my fingers hit up against the leather. It's too small. I've outgrown it. I squeeze my hand into it anyway and look at the Millers' house. Dad has already gone inside.

I run up to the front door and have just put my hand on the doorknob when someone inside opens it for me.

"Hey, little lady. Isn't it way past your bedtime?"

"Little lady?" Come on. "I'm eleven." I have to crane my neck way back to see his face. I thought I had grown a lot lately, but this guy is super-tall. His skin is really tan, and his hair is so blond it's almost white.

"So?"

"Did you have a bedtime the summer you were eleven?"

"Sorry," he says, but he doesn't sound sorry. "I didn't realize eleven was so mature."

He'd better not be the one we're bringing home.

"Do you know where my dad went?"

"They're getting things sorted out downstairs." He turns and walks down the hallway. Maybe he really has to go to the bathroom or something, but he could at least say "Excuse me." Good thing I know where the door to the basement is.

I hear lots of voices as I make my way down the stairs. The Millers must've had the basement redone since last summer. It seems like everyone's house has one of these basement den places except mine. There's a big flat-screen TV up on the wall, with ESPN on mute and a bunch of gigantic guys sprawled out on the couch in front of it. There are so many that some of them have to sit on the floor.

Maybe I don't want a basement den after all. The place stinks. It smells like that one time we picked up Casey's big brother and his friends from football practice. Stinky cheese and feet and the garbage, right before Dad takes it out.

There have to be at least two dozen ballplayers down here, and no windows open to let in some fresh air. A few of the guys look sleepy, and I kind of feel bad for them. My dad is talking to Mr. Miller, who keeps pointing at the different guys and scribbling stuff down on a notepad.

I scan the room for Katie Miller, and I find her before she sees me. She's sitting on one of the couches, between two of the ballplayers. I pretend I don't see her and head straight for the piano. Even though I don't know how to play, I lightly tap my fingers along the keys.

"Do you play?" He has an accent, but I still understand the question.

"Piano?" I ask, turning my face up toward his.

He's two or three heads taller than me, with dark brown skin and brown eyes. He has what my dad calls a five o'clock shadow. I don't know what that means exactly, but his face looks like it could scratch you if you touched it.

He shakes his head. "No. Baseball."

"Not really."

He points to the glove, still on my left hand. I am the worst liar ever.

"I used to play." At least that's not a lie.

"Why don't you play now?" he asks.

But there are too many reasons, and I don't know where to start. I open my mouth and shut it. I do it again. I probably look like a fish.

Finally I say, "It's a long story."

"I like stories. But right now, I like piano." He pulls out the bench and sits on it, patting the spot next to him.

I look around to see who he's trying to get to sit with him, but then he pats the spot again. I sit down and watch as he spreads his hands across the keyboard and starts playing. Softly at first, but then louder. His hands bounce along the keys. Unlike me, he knows what he's doing. I look up at his face and he's smiling, with his eyes closed.

When Haley played flute, I'd sometimes catch her practicing with her eyes closed. Her body would sway to the music. I never told her I watched her. I'm sure she would've been embarrassed.

But this guy whose name I don't know is playing with his eyes closed in front of everyone. He's not afraid or embarrassed. He looks both happy and sad at the same time, if that's possible.

Mr. Miller yells to get everyone's attention, and the guy stops playing. Everyone quiets down and looks at Mr. Miller, who's still scribbling on his notepad. "There were some last-minute changes, but I've got you all paired with your host families. These kind folks are putting you up for the whole summer. That means putting a roof over your head, *not* putting up with your shenanigans. None of that partying you might've gotten used to in college. We're expecting you to obey the house rules."

A few of the players sitting on the floor smile at each other, almost starting to laugh, and then put on straight faces.

"I'm going to read off your names and the names of the families you'll be spending the summer with. Some of these nice folks came out in the middle of the night to pick you up. The others will stop by in the morning. If they're here for you now, they'll wave and find you later. Please raise your hand so they know who you are." He flips through a few pages.

"What's your name?" I whisper to the piano-playing baseball player.

"Hector."

"I'm Quinnen." I don't say that I hope he's going to be staying with us, but I do. All the other guys? Maybe some of them are nice. But are they smiling-with-their-eyes-closed-while-playing-the-piano nice? I don't know.

"Quinnen. You have a nice name."

Dad looks over at me and Hector sitting next to each other, and I think I see him smile. It's only for a second, but I really think he does.

Mr. Miller finally starts to read off the list. "David Hernandez. You'll be staying with me and my family."

A chubby guy with a buzz cut raises his hand. I put my money on him being a catcher.

"Timothy Scott, you're gonna be with Ken and Cathy Montross." *Phew!* That one has lots of tattoos and big, veiny muscles. I'd be scared to run into him in our upstairs hallway at night.

"Hector Padilla," Mr. Miller says. Hector doesn't stick his hand up like he's supposed to. I nudge him and whisper, "Raise your hand."

Please, us. Please, us.

"You're with the Farrells," Mr. Miller says. The Farrells live up the street from us. I look over at Dad, but he's busy talking to one of the players. He doesn't even care which guy we get.

I listen carefully, my eyes darting around the room as Mr. Miller reads out one name after another. One by one, the players raise their hands and smile, like they're happy to be with these families they don't even know.

"Only a few left now, and you'll all be on your way." Mr. Miller flips to the next page.

"Brandon Williams?"

The annoying blond guy who let me in raises his hand.

Not us. Not us, I chant in my head.

"You'll be staying with the Donnelly family."

Dad waves his hand and catches Brandon's eye.

Oh, great.

"Are you tired?" I ask Hector while Mr. Miller finishes reading off the last few names.

"*Sí*," he replies. "Very tired."

"Long flight?"

He nods.

"Where did you come from?" I ask.

"Dominican Republic."

I've looked it up on the map before, since so many good baseball players come from there. "That's really far away." No wonder he's so sleepy.

"Hey, man." I look up and see Brandon walking right toward us. "Hey, little lady. Guess we're going to be seeing a lot more of each other."

I slump on the piano bench. "Yeah."

David Hernandez comes over and says something to Hector in Spanish. Hector stands up. "Are you coming to Opening Day?"

"Always," I say. "See you there. Bye, Hector."

"Good-bye, Quinnen. Maybe sometime I can show you how to throw a slider." He points at my glove. "You're a pitcher, no?"

How does he know?

Something flutters deep inside me, like a knuckleball, but by the time I open my mouth to respond, Hector and David are walking over to their host families and I'm alone with Brandon.

"What position do you play?" I ask Brandon.

"Pitcher."

I cringe as he cracks his knuckles. I hate when boys do that. "How fast's your fastball?"

"Ninety-six. How fast is yours? Like, twenty?" He laughs at his own joke.

I roll my eyes. Katie has her back turned to me, but I can tell she's talking to David. Probably telling him all about her team. *Her team.* It sounds wrong, even when I just say it in my head. Are they undefeated, like last year? I'd ask Casey, but he didn't make the cut this season.

Dad places his hand on my shoulder. "Ready to go?"

Brandon looks down at him. "Mr. Donnelly?"

"That's me." Dad stretches out his hand for a hand-shake. "Nice to meet you, Brandon. Glad to have you around for the summer."

I hate to admit it, but Brandon's arm looks way strong.

Dad has to shake his hand out a little after Brandon lets go. "Let's grab your bags and hit the road. What do you say?"

Dad and I follow Brandon over to a big pile of duffel bags and suitcases. Dad gives me a little smile while Brandon digs through to find his bags. It turns out he packs even more than Mom: three duffels and a wheelie. Does he think he's moving in with us?

Well, he sort of is.

"Do you need some help?" I start to grab one of the bigger duffel bags.

"Hold up." Brandon takes the bag from my hand. "I

don't want these dragging on the ground and getting all scraped up."

"I wasn't going to drag it," I mumble. I wait for Dad to step in. He knows I'm strong enough to carry it. But he doesn't say anything.

With my hand buried deep in my too-small glove, I trail behind Dad and Brandon as we head out to the truck.

They toss Brandon's bags into the back, and I squeeze into the middle seat. I wish my leg wasn't touching Brandon's hairy one, but nobody asked my opinion on the seating arrangement.

"So, Brandon," Dad says, starting up the truck. "What's your story?"

"Where do I start? Well, I grew up in California, north of San Francisco. Marin? Maybe you've heard of it?" He doesn't wait for Dad to say yes or no, just keeps on talking. "Anyway, I was kind of a big deal—lettered in football, basketball, and baseball all four years in high school. I actually got drafted out of high school, but I figured I couldn't pass up a free ride at Stanford."

My favorite third baseman played at Stanford, too. I wonder if he was there at the same time as Brandon. "Hey, do you know—" I try to pipe up.

But Brandon talks right over me. The whole ride home is the life story of Brandon stinking Williams. And the worst part is that Dad's falling for it, smiling and nodding like Brandon is the most fascinating person he's ever met. After Brandon tells us about how he's pretty much the best baseball player ever to play at Stanford—which I seriously doubt—he starts bragging about his girlfriend, Amy, who's in vet school. He even stops to tell me what a vet is—"it's an animal doctor"—like I didn't already know that.

"Honestly, Mr. Donnelly, I appreciate you putting me up and all, but I don't think I'll be here the whole summer. It won't be long until they need me up at Double-A, you know?"

"We'll see," Dad says. "It's pretty stiff competition."

"Yeah," I say. "And do you know how many minor leaguers actually make it to the majors?" I know the answer, but I wonder if Brandon does, or if he's too full of himself and thinks he's a future Cy Young candidate.

"I know the odds; I majored in statistics at Stanford. But those numbers don't matter when you've got the goods."

I grumble and tighten the laces on my glove.

Dad parks the truck in our driveway.

"Your house is huge," Brandon says to me as I hop out of the truck on his side. "Is it just you or— You don't happen to have an older sister, do you?" He raises his eyebrows like a total creep.

I want to smack him with my glove. Dad stands quietly with one of Brandon's bags as my heart beats real loud in my chest.

Dad and I look at each other. Like it's some kind of contest: who will break first?

I know I'll have to tell Brandon, but I don't want to. Why can't Dad be the one to tell someone for once? Why does it always have to be me? Nine months have passed since that day, and Dad can still barely say the words.

"I had an older sister," I tell Brandon. "She passed away."

That's what everyone says, that she "passed away." But it doesn't feel like what happened. It feels like there's this new hole inside of me, and no matter what I do, no matter what anybody says, it'll never be filled.

Brandon's face falls, and for that one second I stop hating him. "I'm sorry," he says, looking me right in the eye. "That stinks."

"Yeah," I say, chewing on my upper lip. "It does."

I help Dad and Brandon carry his luggage up to the guest bedroom, across the hall from mine. Mom put clean sheets on the bed and laid out towels and a fresh toothbrush for Brandon.

"Looks like you're all set," I say. I show him where the bathroom is and where my room is.

He gestures to the closed door in between mine and the guest room. "And that one?"

"That's Haley's room."

He doesn't say anything at first, just looks at me like he's thinking of what he can possibly say. "See you in the morning?"

"Right." I step back into my room and close the door behind me.

I hear Brandon washing up in the bathroom as I crawl back into bed. I open up *Tuck Everlasting*, our sixth-grade summer reading book, but all I want is for my eyes to droop. I want to fall asleep and step into a world like the one in the book, where people can live forever.

But I'm wide-awake, and now I can hear stupid Brandon talking quietly on his stupid cell phone.

I toss my book onto the floor and reach my hand up to tap the wall behind my headboard. Haley and I used to do this every night when I was little, tapping back and forth long after we were supposed to be asleep.

The tune Hector played on the piano is still in my head. I tap it on the wall.

I wait for the tap back. But it never comes.

2

{last summer}

"You've got this, Quinnbear," Haley yelled from the sidelines. I didn't have to turn to look at her. She always sat in that rainbow-striped folding chair down the first-base line, past the bleachers.

I locked eyes with Katie Miller as she made the sign for the next pitch. *Paint the corners, Quinnen. Paint the corners.* Coach Napoli didn't have to say it out loud for me to hear him in my head.

I glanced over to check on the runner on third. He'd better not be thinking about going anywhere. I stared him down, gripping the ball tight in my hand, and focused on the batter.

Wound up and threw.

The batter swung and missed.

"Strike three!" yelled the umpire.

"Panthers advance!" Mr. Miller shouted from the sidelines.

Katie jumped up from her spot behind home plate, ran out toward me, and slapped my outstretched hand hard. "Way to go, QD!"

"Right back atcha, KM!" I'd started calling her KM because there were so many Katies, but also because she had it monogrammed on her backpack. She called me QD, even though I'd never met another Quinnen in my whole life. You had to do something to stick together when you were the only two girls on your Little League team.

Coach had our whole team line up for high fives with the Cardinals. "Good game . . . Good game . . . Good game," we all said to the other team's players. Nobody on the Cardinals was smiling, and we were supposed to keep it under control. Coach said no smiling and celebrating until after they'd left. Can't forget good sportsmanship! After the last high fives, we went back to the Panthers dugout.

"Nice work, everybody," Coach said, scratching his beard. He'd promised he'd keep growing it as long as we kept winning. Pretty soon he'd look like Santa. "Who's up for some ice cream at Gracie's?"

Everyone started yelling and high-fiving each other.

"See you there in fifteen."

I was taking off my cleats when Haley came over.

"Awesome job!" She grabbed my bat and slid it into my bag.

I saw Jaden whisper something into Andrew's ear while Andrew stared at me. Not that dumb stuff again about why I'm playing baseball instead of softball, I hoped. I thought they'd gotten over that by now. And anyway, did it really matter? It wasn't like I was exactly stinking up the joint.

I turned back toward Haley. "Mom couldn't make it?"

Haley shook her head. "She sent me a text: last-minute meeting with the head of the English department. But I'm sure she'll be able to come to your next one."

I kicked off my other shoe, and it banged against the metal fence. Mom always managed to get out of meetings for Haley's recitals. Why couldn't she get out of one for my baseball game?

Casey tapped me on the shoulder. "You want a ride in my car?"

"You mean your mom's car?"

"Right. Her car."

"I'm all set. Haley's giving me a ride. See you at Gracie's."

I slid my bare feet into my flip-flops and followed Haley over to the car.

She turned down the music once we were on the road. "Casey sure seemed anxious to offer you a ride."

"Huh?" I rolled down the window and let the wind move my hand. Mom never let us do this when she was driving. She'd say, "What if a bird swooped in and chomped on your hand?" Haley always laughed and did it anyway.

"Just saying . . ." Haley laughed a little under her breath.

"What? Come on, Hales."

"I'm just saying, maybe Casey . . . Whatever. Like I'm an expert on these things. Only that maybe Casey really wanted you to ride in his car. Next to him. You know?"

"Wait—you think Casey likes me? Gross." I did a real great fake-barf sound.

"Okay, maybe not yet. But someday it's going to be different with you and Casey. You can't be friends with boys forever without it being a little weird."

"But he's Casey!" Casey, who had drawn a beard on his face with marker when Coach started growing his beard. Casey, who wore the same purple sweatshirt almost every day. Casey and I had been friends for as long as I could remember. But I didn't *like* Casey.

"Fine, fine," Haley said. "I'm just trying to share some sisterly wisdom with you. I've got six years on you. That's a lot of wisdom."

I rolled my eyes. "If you have so much wisdom, how come it took you two tries to get your driver's license?"

Haley made a funny sad face back at me. "Wisdom

doesn't guide you through three-point turns. And hey, who are you to dig on your personal chauffeur? You want to walk to Gracie's?"

She said that last bit as we were pulling into the parking lot.

I hopped out of the car and pretended to examine the bumper. "Hales, you dinged it again."

"What?" She walked around the car.

"Made you look!"

"I hope you enjoy the walk home."

I skipped over to the entrance and held the door open for her. "I like the fresh air." That's what Dad always said.

The whole team was spread out over three of the biggest booths inside. Katie waved me over.

"Don't worry about me," Haley said. "I'll grab a cone and sit over in the park across the street until you're done."

"No way. You can sit with the team. You're an honorary Panther."

Haley pulled a stray chair over while Katie and I looked at a menu together. "You want to share a banana split?" Katie asked.

I shook my head. "Fruit doesn't belong with ice cream. Sorry, but no way."

"Quinnen!" Casey shouted from the other side of the table. "I'm going to do it. I'm getting the Grand Slam." The Grand Slam was the biggest sundae

Gracie's offered. Six different flavors of ice cream, plus a brownie, a banana, whipped cream, marshmallow, peanut butter topping, and a cherry on top. If you ate the whole thing, they took your picture and put it up on the wall.

"Eww!" Katie whispered. "I saw someone try that before. It didn't end pretty." She shrank inside her jersey. "I hate it when people barf. If Casey gets a Grand Slam, I can't watch."

"I don't think Coach will let him get it. It's expensive," I said.

Casey pulled out his wallet. It didn't look like the price was going to matter.

The waitress came over and took our orders. Haley and I ordered the Princess Peanut Butter Cup sundae to share. Coach said he'd help Casey out with the Grand Slam, but Casey insisted he could handle it himself. All I could think about was the time Casey ate way too many snacks at the Bandits game last summer and got sick all over Banjo, the mascot. Poor Banjo ended up missing a couple games, and they had to use a squirrel costume while the raccoon one was being cleaned.

Coach went over the plan for our next game. "Now, we can't rely on Quinnen since she pitched the entire game today." He gave me a double thumbs-up, and I returned the favor. "Jordan's got the ball to start. Who remembers who we need to watch out for on the Ravens?"

We talked about the Ravens' best hitters until the waitress came with our sundaes. Casey's Grand Slam was so big it didn't even fit in their biggest bowl. It was on a plate, overflowing onto a tray like they have in the cafeteria at school.

"I can't watch." Katie covered her eyes.

Casey picked up his spoon and dug into the scoop of chocolate ice cream. All the boys near him took out their phones to take "before" pictures.

Haley dangled the cherry from our sundae in front of me, and I grabbed it with my mouth, like a little bird. We always did that—as long as Mom wasn't watching. Mom always said that you're not supposed to play with your food. Me and Haley didn't agree.

I glanced over at Casey. He was halfway through the sundae and he hadn't shared any with Coach. Coach must have gotten up to get his own cone, and based on the bit dribbling down his beard, it looked like he'd gone with strawberry.

"Do you think we should tell him?" I asked Katie, pointing to Coach's ice-cream beard.

"Let's not," she said. I agreed.

I munched on a chunk of peanut butter cup in my ice cream and said to Haley, "Maybe Casey wanted me to ride in his car so he could puke on me."

Haley rolled her eyes.

Katie stuck her fingers in her ears. "Are you guys done talking about puke yet?"

"I hope so." Haley shook her head and pushed the sundae over to me so I could have the last bite.

A few days later, I was up in my room after dinner, lying belly-down on my bed with the summer reading list. I was trying for the billionth time to decide which two books to read, when there was a knock on the door.

I was about to say "Yeah" when Haley bounded in. She kicked off her flip-flops by the foot of my bed, flung herself against my pile of pillows, and let out a huge sigh.

"It was that bad?" Today had been her first day working at the summer camp. Her first day working, period.

"Not bad," she said. "But exhausting." She tucked a stray piece of hair behind her ear as a tiny smile began to spread across her face. She stared past me, at some spot on my wall. "Exhausting *and* amazing."

"Amazing?" I folded up the summer reading sheet and let it fall to the floor. "Amazing how?"

"Just the people, you know? The other counselors. Nobody from school is working there, so everyone's brand-new. All these other people my age from schools around Chicago."

"Nobody you know? That sounds awkward, like being the new kid at school."

"Like *you* know what it's like to be the new kid at school," Haley replied. "We've been here forever. Always in classes with the same people, year after year. When's the last time I met someone new? I can't even remember."

"What about Randol St. Clair? He was new last year."

"Not Randol!" Haley laughed. She'd gotten stuck on a group project with Randol, so he came over to our house a few times in the spring. All he wanted to talk about was Star Wars, even with Mom and Dad. "It's nice to meet people who are . . . different. You know?"

"Like 'Casey' different or like 'Mrs. Wendell' different?" The art teacher Mrs. Wendell had blue hair and every day wore something that had to do with outer space. Planet earrings, night-sky leggings—you name it.

"More 'different' like . . . their very own person. Not like anybody else." The weird smile was back again. "Anyway . . ." She cleared her throat, and just like that the smile disappeared and she looked like normal Haley again. "Did you decide which books you want to read?"

I reached down to the floor for the sheet and handed it to her. I'd put stars next to the ones that sounded interesting, but it wasn't like I was sure. I had a hard time telling if a book was going to be good or not until

I actually read it. Those little one-liners could make any book sound exciting.

"Hmm . . . ," Haley said.

"What?"

"Nothing." Haley got up and grabbed a pen off my desk. She scribbled something down the side of the paper.

"Come on! Let me see." I tried to peek over her shoulder, but she shooed me away. "Hales!"

"Hold on, Q. Sheesh."

I grumbled at her while she kept writing.

Finally she handed the sheet back to me. *Haley's Top Five Books of Fifth Grade.* Beneath her heading, she'd written down five book titles and authors. I compared them to the list the librarian had made.

"None of these are on the list."

"Really? You don't say. . . ." She laughed. "That's why I wrote them down, silly. It's not like your librarian has read all the books in the world. She missed some good ones."

"But I won't get credit for reading those books. It says I have to read two books *from the list.*"

"Whose list?" Haley smiled like she'd won.

"You know which list."

"To be fair, it just says *'the list.'* Kind of vague, don't you think?"

"I don't think Mom's going to be happy if I read two books from your list instead of the books I'm supposed to read."

"Really? Sometimes I don't think you know Mom all that well."

"Haley." I knew Mom just fine. Mom was a rule follower. Dad wasn't one all the time, but Mom sure was.

"Fine." Haley shook her head. "You read the books on the librarian's list. But you know what? You're missing out, my friend."

She stood up and picked at a splatter of blue paint on her khaki shorts.

"I didn't think you were teaching painting," I said.

"I'm not."

"Then how'd you get paint on your shorts?"

Haley took in a deep breath. "Good night, Quinn-bear."

"It's barely bedtime!"

"I know, but I have something I need to talk to Larissa about. And you have some decisions to make." Her eyes shifted to my list, which had fallen to the floor again.

"Night, Hales." She was almost out the door when I said, "Hey, Haley?"

She popped her head back in. "What?"

"See you for breakfast," I said in a little kid voice. Mom said when I was really little, I said that every night to Haley instead of saying good night.

"You're such a dork." Haley laughed, closing the door softly behind her.

I reached down for the summer reading sheet to look at my sister's ideas one more time.

3

{this summer}

"Come on. You have to tell me. What's Brandon like?" Casey asks while his mom backs out of my driveway and starts toward Abbott Memorial Stadium. "Does he eat all the food in your house? Does he have a hot girlfriend? Does he spit sunflower seeds or chew bubble gum? If I was getting paid the big bucks to play baseball, I'd buy as much gum as I wanted. Did you hear he got a million-dollar signing bonus?"

"Casey, sweetie. Give Quinnen a chance to answer one of your questions," his mom says, shaking her head.

"It's—" I start to say.

"I know, it's like . . . it's like living with a movie star, but before he's famous, right?"

"Casey!" I shout.

He finally shuts his mouth and looks at me, giving me a chance to speak.

"It isn't like that at all," I say quietly. "It's . . ."

I think back on the past week since Brandon arrived at our house. It's like my mom turned our house into a bed-and-breakfast. Number of guests: one. But he eats like a family of four. No matter how much Mom tries to tidy up, there's always a bat or a glove or dirty cleats in the hallway. Except now they don't belong to me.

"Brandon's all right. But he never puts the toilet seat down. And he keeps whining about how long it's taking his Xbox to get here. And his legs are really hairy. Like, borderline monster hairy."

"He plays video games?" Casey's eyes widen. "Do you think— Oh man, I can't even believe I'm asking this. Do you think maybe I could come over and hang out with him?"

"Casey!" Mrs. Sanders raises her voice.

"Sorry!" he says. He whispers to me, "Can I come over after the game?"

"I'll have to check with my mom, but yeah, I'm sure you can come."

"I can bring my Xbox! Then he won't have to wait!"

"Totally." I look out the window as we turn into the stadium parking lot. It's the first game of the season. The lot will be full by game time, but Casey wanted to be extra early on Opening Day, so we're one of the first dozen cars here. Mrs. Sanders parks the van in a shady spot and lets us out.

"I'm going to meet up with some folks from the PTA, but I have to take a conference call on my cell first." She says this to both of us, then pulls out some money for Casey. "This is enough to buy a new cap or shirt and food, Case. Please do not spend it all on food. I hope you haven't forgotten what happened two years ago." She gives him her "I'm serious" look.

"I remember," he says.

"Time will tell." Mrs. Sanders looks down at me, and her eyes soften at the corners, like she's remembering the last time the three of us were at the stadium together. "Quinnen, sweetie, here's a little something for you." She presses a folded ten-dollar bill into my hand.

"Thanks, Mrs. Sanders." I wave good-bye and head toward the stadium with Casey. Between the money Mom gave me back at home and the ten dollars from Mrs. Sanders, I definitely have enough for a new Bandits T-shirt now.

"What kind of games do you think Brandon likes to play? I can bring over *Tomb Raider*. Or maybe that new racing game. Or maybe I should just bring over all my games and let him pick."

"Sure." In the back of my head, I wonder if Brandon will even want to play with Casey. But he sure does miss his Xbox.

I scuff my feet in the dry dirt and let Casey talk, talk, talk about Brandon and video games and whether or not the Bandits will win today and what he's going to get from the concession stands.

We walk up to the ticket booth. "Hey there, kiddo," Mrs. Harrington says to Casey. I watch as her eyes shift over to me and her face falls just a bit before she sweeps it back up again into an extra-big smile. Too big. I've gotten used to that. "Hey there, Quinnen! How are you making out?"

I cut in before she says anything about Haley. "Fine. We're hosting this year. We got Brandon."

"Oh!" She looks surprised. "Brandon. I see. How's that going so far?"

I lower my voice. "He thinks he's kind of a hotshot."

Mrs. Harrington lowers her voice to a whisper, too, and leans in toward me. "Now, you didn't hear it from me, but Brandon apparently thought he could get endless free tickets for his buddies. Well, I put the old kibosh on that. Told him it's eight per player. Standard operating procedure." She shakes her head from side to side. "He said he'd check with the manager."

"Sounds like Brandon." I sigh. "But he's okay, I guess."

"Well, you know how it goes, sweetie. If he really *is* a big deal, you won't be stuck with him for too long. Hope he has a great game today!" She winks at me and hands me a ticket. I give her my money, but she pushes it back. "This one's on me."

As we walk over to get food and new Bandits T-shirts, Casey asks, "How come you told Mrs. Harrington that you think Brandon's full of himself but not me?"

"I don't know." But the truth is I do. Ever since Haley died, it's been easier to talk to strangers about things, and way harder to be honest with people I'm actually close to. It's like buried beneath anything I say is something about Haley. Nobody can be real with me, either.

"You really think he's mean?"

"No. I barely know him. He just isn't . . ." *Hector.* Not that I even know Hector that well. But still. He was nice to me. And he didn't treat me like I was some little kid.

"He isn't Haley," Casey says.

I don't say anything back. Casey would never understand. He isn't close to his brother. Scotty treats him like a fly that won't go away. Haley wasn't just my sister. She was my best friend.

I scan the row of food vendors and try to listen to my stomach. The popcorn smells so buttery, but then the pizza with the thick cheese and the spicy sauce sounds so good right now. "Case, what should we get?"

"Pizza." We both say it at the same time.

"Then pizza it is!" I say. That's what Dad always says. Pizza is his favorite.

A whole busload of people must've got in right after

us because the stadium's starting to fill up. The pizza line is the longest one but we still have lots of time before the game starts. I hold our place so Casey can run to get a program and I keep an eye on the players warming up. Most of them are sitting in a circle, stretching. I look for all the guys I saw at the Millers' house, trying to figure out who goes where. In my head, I imagine the batting order. I'm still wondering who will bat leadoff this year when Casey returns with the program.

"I don't think we should get pizza," he says suddenly. "How about hot dogs? It's the first game of the season, and hot dogs are the classic ballpark snack. Pizza would just be wrong."

What's wrong is Casey and his face and the words that are coming out of his mouth. They don't make any sense. When Casey decides what he wants to eat, it's a done deal. He doesn't change his mind. If the restaurant is out of what he wants, he'll whine to his mom and dad until they go somewhere else for it.

"You're nuts. We're getting pizza. Pepperoni pizza. Two slices for five dollars. It's a deal."

He tugs at my arm. "No, seriously. I don't want pizza anymore. I swear. The hot dogs look so good—like the best hot dogs ever."

"It's almost our turn. I'm not going to wait in another line for food. We want to watch batting practice, remember?"

Casey looks like maybe he's having a flashback to

the barf catastrophe and remembering that pizza was the trigger.

"Fine," I say. "You go get hot dogs. I'll get my pizza. We can meet over by the picnic tables behind the out-field."

"Quinnen . . . ," he starts to say, but he can't get it out.

The tall couple in front of us grab their food and move aside. I look up to place my order and open my mouth to talk to the person working the booth.

"I . . . I . . ."

My eyes meet Zack's.

Now I understand why Casey wanted us to buy hot dogs.

Zack's hair isn't spiky anymore. It's cut short. But he still has the lip ring. And he still paints his pinky nails. They're jade. Haley's favorite color.

I can't do it. I can't say anything to him.

I turn and run, leaving behind Casey, leaving behind the line, leaving behind Zack with his mouth open. I bet he doesn't know what to say to me, either.

I don't want pizza. I don't want to eat anything. I run along the chain-link fence that separates the stands from the field, following the first-base line. I don't know if I can ever stop.

What is Zack doing here? How could he get a job at my favorite place on earth? He doesn't even live in town! Didn't he ruin my life enough already?

I don't want to ever see him again. And from the funeral till now, I haven't had to. He lives in the next town over, Hindley. Easy. Don't go to Hindley. Check. Done.

I sit down against the wooden wall behind center field. It's as far away as I can get from Zack, from everyone, from everything, without leaving the ballpark. I pull out fistfuls of grass until underneath my nails is tinged green and full of dirt.

This is mine. My place. The only place that's not ruined. Nothing bad is supposed to happen here. Doesn't he know that?

Hot tears spill down my cheeks.

I consider calling *After Midnight* tonight with a request for a song telling Zack to get lost. But I can't think of any mean songs, and they probably wouldn't play the request. But maybe the guy who hosts the show would just listen to me.

I pull out a few more chunks of grass. *That's a stupid idea.*

"Quinnen!"

Whoever is calling my name doesn't sound like Casey. The voice is too deep, and it has an accent.

I stand on my tiptoes to look into center field. It's someone in a baseball uniform, running toward me.

Hector.

I wipe the tears off my face. I'm probably all dirty and grass-stained by now. I rub under my eyes with my T-shirt. A tiny door in the middle of the center-field wall opens up, and Hector comes through.

"I didn't know they had a door there."

He closes it softly behind him. "Why were you running?"

"I saw someone. Someone I wasn't expecting to see. This guy who ruined my life."

"Oh," Hector says. "Your life, it's ruined? Already? Who is this person; what'd he do?"

"It's a long story. You probably don't have time for it."

They're testing the microphone for the national anthem. Hector opens the door for a peek and sits down on the grass next to me. "I have one minute. Maybe two. Brandon's pretty nervous about his first game, you know?"

I look up at Hector. "Brandon? Nervous?"

"Un poco." Hector holds his thumb and index finger an inch apart.

"I didn't think anything could make Brandon nervous." I stop playing with the grass in front of me and look through the open door at the field.

"Maybe he'll surprise you. Everyone is nervous or scared sometimes. Even Brandon."

"It's probably been a minute. I don't want to get you in trouble before you even get to play."

Hector nods. "Will you come back to the game now? For Brandon?" He waits. "For me?"

"Okay," I say, standing up. My legs get a little shaky when I think about seeing Zack. What if he's one of the people who walk and up down the aisles during the game, selling stuff? "Good luck."

"I'll need luck later this week. Today is easy. No pitching for me today." Hector has to duck to get through the door. Before closing it, he sticks his head back through again. "Good luck to you."

As I start walking back to the bleachers along the first-base line, I begin formulating my plan. If Zack thinks he can come here and sell pizza, so what? I don't need to visit the concession stands. I can bring my own snacks or ask Casey to get my food for me.

When I get to our seats, Casey is waiting with two hot dogs. Actually, what used to be two hot dogs. Two hot dog holders and some dirty napkins rest in my seat.

"Sorry." Casey moves them out of the way. "They were getting cold, and I didn't know what to do."

I take off my Bandits cap and turn toward the field for the national anthem.

"Are you okay? With Zack and everything? Do you want me to go get you another hot dog? Or a lemon ice?"

I know Casey's trying, but he doesn't get it. A new hot dog won't fix anything. "Don't worry about the hot dogs. I'm not that hungry."

4

{last summer}

I was helping Mom set the kitchen table for dinner. Dad was picking Haley up from the camp and they'd be home any minute. I had just put down all the silverware when the door connecting the kitchen to the garage opened.

"Hey, Mom? Is it all right if we have one more for dinner?" Haley asked, popping her head in.

Mom was too busy stirring spaghetti sauce on the stove to turn around. "Is Larissa coming over?" During the school year, Haley's friend Larissa joined us for dinner when she and Haley worked on homework together. I think she liked my mom's cooking more than she liked her own mom's.

But that night it wasn't Larissa. Haley stepped into the kitchen with a boy. No, not a boy. A . . . guy? He was tall—taller than my sister but not baseball-pitcher tall. His dark brown hair was spiky, and he had an eyebrow ring. And was there something sticking out of his mouth—a lip ring? Were they having a sale when he went to get his eyebrow pierced?

"Zack's grandma is out of town, so Dad and I invited him over for dinner. Is that okay?"

It looked like Zack hadn't even washed his hands after camp, unless he'd painted his pinky nail on purpose.

"Sure," Mom said. "There's plenty of food to go around. Quinnen, can you set a place for Zack, please?"

At least Mom remembered about me. Haley didn't introduce me to Zack. I'd never even heard of him before, and I knew all of Haley's friends.

Our kitchen table wasn't very big. If I'd known we were going to have five people, not the usual four, I would have set the dining room table. That's what we always did when Larissa stayed for dinner. I grabbed a fifth plate and silverware and squeezed in a spot at the kitchen table for Zack.

"I'm going to change real quick before dinner," Haley said. "Quinnen, you can keep Zack entertained, right?" She scooted out of the kitchen before I had a chance to reply.

Zack gave me a little wave. The nail paint had to be on purpose because it was on both of his pinkies. "Hey," he said. "I don't think we've officially met yet."

"Hi." I couldn't stop myself from staring at his lip

ring and wondering how it felt. Did it get in the way when he was eating? Or brushing his teeth? Did it ever get stuck on his clothes when he was getting dressed in the morning?

"So you're Haley's little sister."

"I'm Haley's *only* sister."

"Right." He caught my mom's eye. "Is there anything I can do to help?"

"We're just about ready to eat, so grab a spot at the table. Make yourself at home. Can I get you something to drink?"

Zack sat down in the seat that Haley usually sat in. Haley came back into the kitchen. She'd changed into one of her polo dresses and smelled like citrus perfume. She'd put on earrings, too. They were so big and dangly I wasn't sure if they were earrings or Christmas tree ornaments. You couldn't pay me to let someone poke a hole through my ears. No thanks.

Haley sat right down in the chair next to Zack and tucked her hair behind her ear, like she was hoping he'd notice her earrings, too.

"Hey, that's my seat," I said. I always sat there. It was the closest to the fridge, in case I needed seconds on milk.

"I'm sorry. Did you want to sit next to Zack?" Haley raised her eyebrows at me. She shot me a look that said, What is up with you?

I shook my head and slid into the seat next to Mom.

It felt like we were playing musical chairs. When Mom served the spaghetti, I didn't get as much as I wanted since we had to make one more serving for Zack. And was I the only one who noticed there were just four rolls? Mom cut them in half so it wasn't as obvious. But I could still tell. It's more than a little rude not to give advance warning when you're bringing someone over.

"This is Zack's first summer working at the camp, too," Haley said.

"How do you like it so far?" Dad asked as he buttered his roll.

Zack finished chewing a mouthful of spaghetti before answering. "I love it. The kids are great. They have so much energy, and they love all the different art projects we've been doing. We're working on a mural this week."

"I always wished Quinnen would give that camp a try," Mom said. "It's nice having a camp with an arts focus so close by. They're hard to find these days."

"We still have some spots for sessions later this summer." Zack smiled at me, and I wondered what would happen if he got a string of spaghetti stuck in his lip ring. Casey would totally do that if he had a lip ring.

"What do you think, Quinnen?" Mom asked.

Did I really have to remind her *again*? "Mom, I have baseball. Practice and games and, if we keep winning, the tournament—remember? In Indiana? I don't have time for art camp."

"I wasn't suggesting it instead of baseball but in addition to, honey. It doesn't hurt to be well rounded." She turned to Zack. "Maybe next summer," she said.

I'll have baseball next summer, too. Mom didn't catch me shaking my head. Sometimes I wasn't sure she really got it: how important it was to focus on the one thing you really wanted. That's what all the big leaguers did. They lived and breathed baseball from before they were my age.

Haley twirled some spaghetti on her fork. "You know how I was telling you about that amazing book by Junot Díaz that I was reading last week?"

Mom nodded.

"Zack lent me the book. He's super into Junot Díaz. Díaz is, like, one of your favorite authors, right?" Haley looked at Zack as she said that last bit, and popped a bite of spaghetti in her mouth.

"That's fantastic," Mom said, leaning the tiniest bit toward Zack. "It's always been so important to me as an English instructor to expose my girls to all kinds of literature. Now, tell me, Zack, what other authors have you been enjoying lately?"

Zack was chewing his roll then, so he couldn't answer right away.

I didn't know how he could do it. Just jump right in, squeeze his way into this table, and fit in like he'd been here forever. He even had Mom swooning over him. And that's not easy. Trust me, I'd tried.

"I read a book by her, too. By that Juno lady," I piped up.

Haley stifled a laugh and looked at me funny. "Really?"

It felt like everyone was staring at me. Mom and Dad and Haley and Zack and his dumb lip ring. Somehow he was still chewing on that bite of roll. I didn't think it was humanly possible to chew a roll for that long. "I read it at the school library one day."

Mom stood up to clear the plates, and Zack got up to help her.

"It's okay if you don't know what we're talking about," Haley said to me quietly.

"But I do know," I said. "You and Mom aren't the only ones who read!" I pushed my chair—no, not even *my* chair, because Haley was in *my* chair—back hard. It squeaked on the floor.

"Quinnen!" Mom sounded annoyed.

"Sorry."

Haley whispered. "If you had actually read it, you'd know that Junot Díaz is a guy."

I saw Zack turn his head when she said it.

I could feel my cheeks growing redder and redder as I put my plate in the dishwasher. It scraped against the little poky things that held in the dishes. *Just because I don't get an A+ in ELA doesn't mean I'm not a reader,* I thought. *How can they know everything I've read? They can't prove it.*

Even though Mom and Zack had the dishes under control, Haley and Dad stayed to hang out in the kitchen. It seemed like Mom and Dad were playing Twenty Questions with Zack—only Zack didn't seem to mind. Nobody asked: Hey, Quinnen, do you have any questions for Zack? Nobody asked: Hey, Quinnen, how was baseball practice this afternoon?

So I shouldn't have been surprised that none of them noticed when I grabbed my glove and ball and went out through the garage into the backyard.

It was that point in the summer when the days were still super-long. Even after dinnertime, the sun wasn't close to setting. I tossed some balls high into the sky to warm up my arm. I loved the *thwump* the ball made when it hit my glove. Steady and predictable. No matter what, baseball was always there. Okay, sure, it disappeared in the winter, but it came back every spring. Like clockwork, Dad said.

I could see into the kitchen through the window over the sink. It looked like they had mostly finished cleaning up. Now it was just Mom in the window. She gave me a little wave. I nodded to let her know I could see her, but I didn't take my hand out of my glove. When I got bored with tossing pop-ups, I dragged out the backstop to practice pitching at a target. *Blam. Blam. Blam.* Three strikes. You're out.

My arm felt a little stiff, so I sat down on the grass to try some of the new stretches Coach had taught us. Upstairs, the light in Haley's bedroom turned on. I guessed someone had already come by to get Zack. I reached my right arm over my back and tucked the other arm under and around, locking my hands together. I could do this stretch easy at practice, but some of the other kids on my team needed a strap.

My hands were still all locked together like that when I looked up at Haley's window again.

I was wrong. Nobody had come by to get him. Zack was in Haley's room. Zack was alone with Haley in her room.

And they were kissing.

Right in the window, where anybody—okay, I— could see.

He was kissing my sister. Zack with his dumb lip ring was kissing my sister.

And until today, I didn't even know about him.

I thought Haley told me everything. I knew about every quiz she took in school and how she did on it, every time Larissa said something that hurt Haley's feelings, every time Haley was upset or worried or sad or happy or mad. I thought I knew my sister, inside and out.

But I didn't know about Zack.

Haley hadn't told me.

5

{this summer}

I reach into the cupboard for my favorite granola. The box feels suspiciously light. Too light.

"Brandon," I mutter.

I glance over at the world's biggest eater, sitting at the kitchen table with Mom. Dad is standing at the counter with his laptop, answering emails and scarfing down a bagel before heading off to work. Mom is quietly reading the paper while Brandon's playing some game on his phone, with the sound all bleeping and blooping, and drinking coffee. He's sitting in Dad's chair. Haley's chair is empty.

In front of Brandon is an empty cereal bowl. How many bowls did he manage to scarf down before I woke up this morning? Three? Five? *Thirty?*

I pull the box down to confirm what I'm pretty sure I already know. I reach inside and pull out a plastic bag with only crumbs in it.

Sighing loudly, I crumple up the bag and toss it in the trash can. Nobody looks up. Not Mom, not Dad, not Brandon, either. They're all lost in their own worlds, their own little bubbles.

I peek inside the cabinet to see what cereals Brandon hasn't finished off yet. The only thing left is an old box of Cheerios. After pouring myself a bowl, and adding what's left of the milk in the fridge—barely a few spoonfuls—I sit down in my seat. At least he left me that.

"Hey, Quinnen?"

I look up when Brandon speaks, my mouth full of stale Cheerios. "Yeah?"

"Some of the guys are coming over pretty soon. It's kind of a team thing, you know? You think you can give us some space?"

I'm still hanging on the first part—some of the Bandits coming over to our house, maybe even Hector—when the last part hits me. I'm not allowed. Not invited. *At my own house.*

I look for Mom to raise her eyes up over the paper. To step in and say that this is my house, too. That it was my house first. But she just flips the page. Worse: Dad keeps typing away like Brandon didn't say anything to me.

"Dad?"

He stops typing and glances at the clock. "Shoot. I'm going to be late." He wraps the last bit of his bagel in a paper towel. "Have fun today, kiddo." He ruffles my hair and gives Mom a little kiss on the top of her head, and then he's gone.

It's just me and Mom and Brandon. Dad always used to stick up for me. Always. We used to be a team.

"Quinnen? You understand what I'm saying?" Brandon looks up from his cell phone.

"I understand," I say, and pop another spoonful of stale Cheerios in my mouth.

I'm putting my cereal bowl into the dishwasher, peeking out the window at Brandon, Hector, and the other starting pitchers hanging around the picnic table in the backyard, when Mom gets up from the table. "Hey, Quinnen?"

"Yeah." I close the dishwasher.

"I'm sorry to spring this on you at the last minute, but you know how I've been reading a lot this summer?"

I nod. *This summer?* Ever since Mom decided not to go back to work last September, all she's done is read. Sometimes I wonder if she's actually reading those books, or if she's just flipping the pages, thinking about Haley and all the books she wanted to read that she'll never get to.

She picks up something from the top of the micro-wave. "I signed us up for a mother-daughter book club that Mrs. Hennigan from down the street is hosting. The first meeting is next Wednesday."

She hands me a book: *Are You There God? It's Me, Margaret.* The cover has some girl's feet with all the toenails perfectly painted. *So, it's about God and feet?*

"No way. I'd have to read the whole thing in a week?"

"It's okay if you can't read it all in time for the meeting. It was a bit of a last-minute decision."

Why didn't Mom even ask me if I wanted to do the book club in the first place? Mrs. Sanders would have asked. She wouldn't just make Casey do something like this.

I turn the book over to read the back cover, and flip through some of the pages. Periods? Training bras? "This book is gross! You want me to read it and then talk about it with a bunch of strangers?" I push it back into her hands.

"Not strangers. Friends. And me." Mom takes the book from me. "Calm down, Quinnen."

"You don't get it. I don't want to talk about books with you or your friends or their daughters. I'm *not* Haley."

Mom cringes. She hardly ever says her name any-more. Nobody does. It's like they want to pretend she never existed.

"Quinnen," Mom says. But then she just stands there.

She could never talk to me about books. Or training bras and periods. Girl talk was what she did with Haley. They would sit around and paint each other's toenails and fingernails. Like the girly girl on the book's cover.

"I'm not doing it."

I hustle out of the kitchen and stomp up the stairs and into my room. I close the door tight. I figure Mom'll come up after me. She always does. She never leaves me alone.

But I wait and I wait. This time she doesn't come.

Brandon, Hector, and the three other starting pitchers are still out in the backyard an hour later when Mom knocks on my door. I've got my bedroom window open so I can listen in. "I'm going to run some errands. Do you want to come along for the ride?"

If I didn't think I'd get in trouble, I'd shush Mom so I could hear them better. These guys know even more about baseball than Coach Napoli. There's so much I could learn from them.

"No thanks," I say. "I was hoping the other guys would leave and then I could hang out with Brandon and Hector."

Mom opens the door. "Didn't Brandon ask you to

give him some space when he's with his friends? You need to respect his wishes."

"Yeah, but . . ." I don't think Brandon would mind if it was just him and Hector.

"I know Brandon's staying with us, but your whole summer shouldn't revolve around the Bandits." Mom taps her fingers on the door. "You need to find something else to keep yourself busy."

Something else to replace baseball. I wish she would just come out and say it. But nobody says what they really think anymore. If we did, we'd talk about Haley all the time. At least, I would.

"I'll see if Casey wants to come over." Casey can keep anyone busy.

"All right." Mom closes my bedroom door softly behind her.

I watch through the front window as Mom's car pulls out of the driveway and heads down the road, and then I go downstairs. In the living room, there's this whole wall of bookshelves. Most of the books are Mom's and Dad's, but a few years ago Haley started putting her old books down here to make room for her newer ones upstairs.

When I was little, Haley used to read to me. Not just the books that were for kids my age but also the parts she liked from her books. She wanted to be a writer and work for a big magazine in New York City. People thought she wanted to be a writer so she could be famous, but I know that wasn't it. Haley wanted to see the world. She wanted to get out of here.

Haley's books are organized by author. Such a Mom thing, but it was a Haley thing, too. I run my finger along the spines. Alcott. Avi. Babbitt. Balliett. Bauer. Birdsall.

Blume.

She has three books by Judy Blume. *Forever* . . . and *Deenie* and—there it is—*Are You There God? It's Me, Margaret.* I pull it out. It's smaller than the copy Mom tried to give me, and it looks different. This one is purple, and it has a bra on the cover.

Haley read this book. Did she read it when she was my age? I try to think of all the books I ever saw her read, but there were too many of them.

If Haley read this when she was my age, then how old was I when she read it? Haley was six years older than me, so five. I was five when Haley read it.

That was a really long time ago.

There's a knock at the front door. I don't want to put the book back yet, so I shove it under my T-shirt and go to see who's there. I open it and find Casey, the mind reader.

"I got a new Xbox game and I wondered if Brandon wanted to play now that his Xbox is here."

"*Hi*, Casey," I say. "I was about to call you."

"Oh, right. Hi. Anyway, is Brandon around?" He peeks around the room like I've stashed Brandon somewhere and his feet might be sticking out from under the curtains.

Sometimes it feels like ever since Brandon came here, I've been invisible. Even to Casey.

"He's out back with some of the Bandits. You didn't hear them when you walked over?"

"Nope."

We head out back through the sliding glass door in the living room. It's probably okay if Casey does the bothering.

"Why are you holding your stomach like that?" Casey asks.

It turns out most of the guys have left anyway; it's just Brandon and Hector sitting at the picnic table now.

"I pulled a muscle."

"A stomach muscle? How did you do that? You don't even play— I mean . . ."

"Forget about it."

Casey forgets about it, all right. He runs right over to Brandon to show him the game. I don't think he'd notice if I disappeared into the cornfields behind my house.

I walk over to Hector. He's staring at this white sheet of paper covered in numbers. Stats for the batters he's going to face tomorrow? I wonder. "Hey, Hector."

He looks up at me. "Hey, Quinnen. Are you coming to my game tomorrow?"

"Of course," I say. "Are you nervous?"

Hector nods. "Always a little nervous before the first game in a new place." He points at my stomach. "What's that under your shirt?"

I check to see if Brandon or Casey is looking. They're still busy, so I slide the book out and hand it to Hector. "It was my sister's."

He looks at the front and back covers, flips through some of the pages. "You like to read?" He hands the book back to me.

"Not really. My mom wants me to join this book club. A *mother-daughter* book club. I'd rather eat a turd." I can't help sticking my tongue out of the corner of my mouth after I say it.

"What is a *turd*?" he asks.

I laugh. "Um . . . like, in the toilet," I say. "Poop."

"*Caca?*"

"Yeah," I say. Some Spanish, it turns out, is very easy to understand.

Casey grabs the book out of my hand.

"Jeez, Case!" I try to snatch it back, but he's too quick.

"Whoa! Sexy mama!"

"Gross. Come on. Give it back!" I say, blushing.

"Whatcha got there?" Brandon asks. Casey holds up the book to show him. I want to crawl under the picnic table and never come out. "Nice. I remember when my sister read it. 'Dear God. It's me, Margaret.

Can you help me buy a bra?'" He says it in this stupid falsetto.

Where is my feisty sister when I need her? Haley would swoop in here and dazzle Brandon by saying something clever. Or at least grab the book out of his hands and smack him with it. Okay, maybe she wouldn't have done either of those things. But she wouldn't have stood there laughing at me, either.

Now I don't have anyone to stand up for me.

Even Casey isn't on my side anymore. He's on Team Brandon.

My eyes are starting to tear up when Hector stands up fast.

Casey looks on like maybe there's going to be a fight, but Hector doesn't touch Brandon at all. He snaps the book right out of Brandon's hands before he even knows what's going on.

"Stop it," Hector says.

He's usually so calm. The surprise of it makes the rest of us get real quiet.

"Stop being a turd," he says.

Casey falls over laughing. Big belly laughs. He can't even stop himself, he's laughing so hard. He's going to get grass stains all over his white shirt. "He called . . ." He can only get that much out before cracking up again. He looks up at Brandon. "He called you a *turd*."

Brandon rolls his eyes, like it's not funny at all.

I'm not surprised. Turds don't usually have a sense of humor.

"Thank you," I whisper to Hector as he hands Haley's book back to me.

6

{last summer}

"Haley, come on. I can't be late!" I yelled up the stairs. My baseball glove was on my hand. I was ready for my game. All I needed was for Haley to be ready, too.

"Haley!" I yelled again.

"Coming!" she finally shouted back. I heard her door slam and the slapping of her bare feet on the hardwood floor.

As she came down the stairs, I could see why it had taken her so long. She had changed her clothes. Earlier, she'd had on her normal T-shirt and shorts, but she'd replaced them with a jean miniskirt and a tank top that looked like it was a size too small. Plus she had put some kind of glittery makeup all over her eyes.

"Why are you all dressed up?" I asked. "It's just a baseball game."

"I'm not," she said, grabbing her car keys off the hook by the door and slipping into a pair of flip-flops. "Come on. Didn't you say we needed to go?"

Yes, you are, I wanted to say back. But I didn't.

The whole ride to the baseball field, Haley's phone kept buzzing and buzzing inside her bag. "Who keeps calling you?" I finally asked when we were stopped at a red light.

"Probably Zack. He's going to meet me at the game."

"Zack's coming to my game?"

"Yeah," she said. "Is that a problem or something?"

"No," I said quietly. I stared at the car in front of us. There were a lot of bumper stickers on the back. There was even that funny one boasting about how the driver's kindergartener is on the honor roll; Mom really liked that one. But it didn't seem so funny right then.

"Real convincing," Haley said.

"Why do you like him so much?" It was something I'd been thinking about since that night two weeks earlier when he'd come over for dinner. He called Haley on the phone all the time, but I couldn't figure out how they could talk so much. Didn't they see each other every day at camp? What did she have to tell him? What we ate for dinner? What toothpaste she used?

"There are lots of reasons," she said. "I mean, he's artistic and he's smart. He really thinks about things,

58

you know? He doesn't just do what everyone else is doing because that's what you're supposed to do." She got that one right. Zack was the only person I knew with a lip ring who wasn't in some band on TV. "I thought you'd like him." She tapped her fingers on the steering wheel.

Is she waiting for me to say that I do? That I like Zack, too? Am I supposed to lie?

"Oh," I said. "Is Zack . . . is he your boyfriend?"

"I'm not sure yet," she said. "But maybe soon."

"Let's go, Panthers, let's go!" Katie and I sat next to each other on the bench, slapping our laps and clapping our hands as we did our cheer. "Let's go, Panthers, let's go!" *Clap, clap.* One of the best hitters on our team, Joe, was batting, and Casey was on third, ready to score if Joe could get a hit.

"Come on, Joe!" Katie yelled.

If Casey scored, we'd have the lead again. We kept going back and forth with the Orioles, but we were running out of innings. We needed to score the go-ahead run and then shut them down. A win's a win, Coach always said. No arguing with that.

Joe swung and missed. Strike three. Two outs.

"Go get 'em, QD," Katie whisper-yelled. I grabbed my bat and made my way to the on-deck circle while Tommy Sullivan stepped up to the plate. I took a few

practice swings and looked out to where Haley and Zack were sitting.

They weren't there.

Haley's rainbow chair was there, and Zack's Chicago Bears fold-up chair was there, but both were empty. *Maybe they went to the bathroom,* I told myself. *They'll be back by the time I get up to bat. If I get to bat . . .*

"Let's go, Tommy, let's go!" Katie and the others cheered from the bench. I took another practice swing. I was ready.

"Come on, Tommy," I said. "You've got this." The Orioles pitcher was one pitch away from walking him. It'd be awesome for Tommy to get a hit right now and give us the lead, but a tiny part of me wanted it to be me who got the big hit.

Tommy stood there as the pitch came in. The Orioles catcher jumped up to catch it. Way too high. Ball four.

Tommy took first base. Casey stayed at third.

"Let's go, QD!" Katie yelled. She let out a huge whistle as I stepped into the batter's box.

You've got this, I told myself. *You've got this.*

"There's *two* girls on your team?" the Orioles catcher asked through his mask.

"Yeah," I answered, digging my heels into the dirt, holding my bat back behind my head. "Wait—you just figured that out now?"

The pitcher wound up and threw.

I didn't budge an inch. Way outside.

"Ball one!" the umpire called.

"Come on, Quinnen. Crush it." That was Coach Napoli. I didn't have to look to know he was twiddling his beard. He always did that during close games.

I choked up on my bat as the pitcher wound up again. I didn't swing at that one, either; it was high and outside. "Ball two!" the umpire said.

I stepped out of the batter's box to adjust my gloves and glanced over at where Haley and Zack should be. How long could Haley be in the bathroom? It was a porta-potty! She always cheered for me when I was batting, even when we were creaming the other team. And I always heard her loudest of anyone when it was close, when my at-bats really mattered.

I checked the on-deck circle. Kyle Monaghan was there. I liked Kyle all right, but he was one of the worst batters on our team. I needed more than a walk. I needed a hit. I stepped back into the batter's box and gripped the bat tight. *Be ready to swing away, QD.*

The pitcher stepped forward and hurled the next pitch. It probably wasn't a strike, but that didn't matter. I reached out for it and hit it hard with the barrel of the bat. The ball found the gap between the first baseman and the second baseman and kept going. I was running. Rounding first base, going for second. I could hear the team cheering as Casey scored and then as Tommy beat the throw to the plate. I stopped at third, panting. *We did it! I did it! We have the lead again! Panthers rule!*

I took off my batting gloves and tucked them in my pocket. And then I looked over to where Haley was supposed to be. Her rainbow-striped chair was still empty.

She'd missed it.

"Great game, everybody. I wish I could take you all out for ice cream today, but you just keep winning, and I'm going broke. See you at practice on Tuesday." Coach fake-saluted, and then all of us players started talking at the same time.

"Want to come over to my house?" Katie asked me. "We can do flips on the trampoline."

"I wish I could," I said. "Tonight's family dinner, though. Mom's idea."

Katie sighed loudly. "Moms."

"Tell me about it. Have your neighbor make a video and send it to me if you can do ten in a row."

"Of course!" She waved good-bye, and I walked over to where we hung up the bats. I wanted to bring mine home so I could practice hitting with Dad over the weekend.

"Nice game." I looked up and saw Zack. He was holding hands with Haley.

"Thanks," I mumbled. I pretended I couldn't tell

which bat was mine and took an extra-long time to find it.

When I finally grabbed it, Zack and Haley weren't holding hands anymore. Haley's hand was touching something on her neck. There was a splotch there, a purple-red spot. There's no way that was there before. I would have seen it in the car.

"What happened to your neck?" I reached out my finger to point at the spot.

"It's nothing," she said.

I shook my head. "Come on. What is it?"

"You wouldn't understand. I'll explain later."

I hated when she said that. If she knew, she should tell me. We didn't used to keep secrets from each other. But now I didn't know how many secrets she was keeping from me, how many things I would have to wait to find out. I had lost track.

She went to grab my bag, but I shooed her off. "I've got it," I said.

"We're giving Zack a ride home. Come on. I don't want to be late."

We? Right, Haley.

Zack carried both their chairs as we walked back to the car.

"I don't know what's up with you," Haley said as I put my stuff in the trunk. "Your team won. Why are you in such a bad mood?"

I shrugged.

She was right. We'd won. My team had won, and I'd come through with the most important hit of the whole game. The winning hit.

But she'd missed it because she was off doing something with Zack, and she wouldn't even tell me about it.

7

{this summer}

It's the day of Hector's first scheduled start at Abbott Memorial Stadium, and Casey and I are walking over to the concession stands like we always do before the game. Suddenly I freeze. My legs feel like they're made of cement, and the hunger I felt on the car ride to the stadium vanishes. I don't want to eat anything. Not from the concession stands, at least.

"Quinnen, come on!" Casey yells.

"I'm going to go sit down," I say, but it comes out a near whisper. "I don't feel so great."

"But the game's starting soon. We gotta get food now or—" He remembers. "Can I buy something for you?"

"As long as you don't eat it first."

Casey glares at me but then breaks into a smile.

"A hot dog and fries." I hand him the crumpled ten from my pocket.

"I'm not gonna do this for you forever. You know, you can't keep avoiding him."

"Yeah, I can." I walk to our seats, my heart calming down with each step I take away from the smells I love and the person I hate.

Banjo stops by and gets me to rub his furry raccoon belly while I wait for Casey. Ten minutes later, Casey arrives with a huge soda, a hot dog, and fries for me and corn on the cob, a tuna sandwich, and bottled water for him.

"They sell tuna sandwiches here? I don't remember ever seeing them for sale. They aren't even fried."

"There's a new booth this year," he says. "With healthy food where they take out the *wu-tang* and don't put any sugar in."

"Take out the *wu-tang?*"

"Isn't that what they call it? It makes you go crazy, and it makes some people sick." He shakes his head. "I don't know. My mom thinks I shouldn't have so much *wu-tang* anymore."

"I think it's called *gluten*. You sure you don't want some fries?" I dangle one in front of his face. It has so much salt on it that it sparkles.

"Stop it. Of course I want one."

"Then why can't you have one?"

Casey doesn't say anything at first. He takes the wrapper off his sandwich. "Mom doesn't want me to end up looking like Pablo Sandoval."

"But he's such a good hitter."

"I know. It's okay, though. I'd rather look like Hector or Brandon. I bet they eat real healthy and work out all the time."

I don't tell him that Brandon eats more than anyone I've ever met.

The loudspeaker squeaks. "Attention. Would Quinnen Donnelly please come to the information booth?"

I bolt out of my seat. "Hold this." I practically throw my hot dog onto Casey's lap before running over to the information booth, my heart beating so loud in my chest it might as well be broadcast over the speakers. My legs are shaking when I get there.

"Quinnen! Just the young lady we were looking for," says the woman wearing a nice Bandits polo shirt. She's smiling and waving at me.

"What's wrong? Did my mom call?"

"'What's wrong?'" She looks confused. "Oh, sweetie. I'm so sorry. I probably gave you a heart attack. Our volunteer to read the starting lineup is tied up in traffic and he's not going to make it in time. We thought perhaps you'd like to help us out today."

Her words are like someone strapping an oxygen mask over my face. I can breathe again. Even though I've been singled out a million times before and it's never been a big deal, after last summer I can only think of one reason for someone to call out my name on the loudspeaker: something bad happening to someone I love.

I take a deep breath. "Sure." I smile back at her so she knows I'm fine. *You're going to read the starting lineup*, I tell myself. *It's okay.*

I follow her up the stairs to the announcer's booth, behind home plate. The announcer is staring out a big window with the most perfect view of the diamond. There's a lady next to him with stacks of papers she keeps shuffling and handing to him. She talks really fast, like she's had one too many Red Bulls. In the back of the room, there are shelves with more Bandits stuffed animals, pennants, and doodads than I would know what to do with. Well, if somebody offered, they'd probably fit in my room.

"You've done this before, right?" the announcer asks, handing me a sheet of paper.

"Yeah," I say, looking over the list of names. "I've got it."

"You're on in five," the too-much-Red-Bull lady says, pointing at us.

I read the names softly to myself. But when I get to the bottom of the page, I realize they left one off: Hector's.

"Excuse me," I say to the announcer. "Do I get to say the pitcher's name?"

"Normally I like to add my own special intro for the pitcher."

"Please?"

"Oh, okay. Sure. Why not, kiddo? Just keep it under twenty seconds. They've got a starting time to make."

Before I know it, we're getting the three-two-one countdown, and the announcer is saying, "And here it is, your starting lineup for the Tri-City Bandits, read by our very own . . . Quinnen Donnelly!"

He points to me, and I read the whole lineup without any mistakes—I hope. Then I put on my very best announcer voice for the finale. "And tonight's starting pitcher, number fifteen, making his first start for the Bandits . . . Hector Padilla!"

Cheers fill the stadium. I know they're not for me reading the lineup, but still—there's something magical about baseball time. Everything just feels right.

"Great job," the announcer says to me. "You're a natural. You even knew how to pronounce Hector's last name. Pa-*dee*-uh. You want to watch the top of the inning from up here? Best seat in the house."

I think about Casey down in our seats and my hot dog. It's probably in Casey's stomach by now, whether it has any gluten in it or not. "Okay." I sit back down in the bouncy swivel chair.

The first batter for the Cardinals takes a few swings outside the batter's box. He looks strong and mean, but I bet he's no match for Hector.

Hector winds up and throws one that catches the inside corner. The batter can't get his bat around fast enough. "Striiiike one."

"Come on, Hector. You've got 'em," I whisper.

He winds up and throws. The pitch looks low but maybe on the edge of the strike zone. I have to wait for the umpire to know for sure. "Striiiiike two," the announcer says.

I turn to give him a thumbs-up. "I know him. I know Hector. He's my friend." The announcer smiles at me like I'm a little kid. Like, *Oh sure. Hector's her friend, and I'm best buddies with the president.*

Hector shakes off the catcher and winds up. He throws, and the batter swings. All I hear is the sound of the ball hitting the bat. The next thing I see is Hector, crumpled over, down on the ground.

The announcer puts his hand over the red mute button and swears.

"Where did it hit him?" I ask.

The announcer shakes his head. It all happened so fast.

Someone's rushing out onto the field—I think it's the manager—and someone's following with a stretcher.

Hector's not moving.

He's not moving.

He's not moving.

But I am. I run out of the booth and down the stairs, not even looking where my feet land. I am flying.

"Hector!" I yell.

When I get to the fence around the field, I remember to breathe.

"Sorry, miss, but we can't allow you on the field right now," the security guard tells me.

"But—"

"Are you family?"

"No. Nobody is. Hector's family doesn't live here."

Hector is still lying down, and there's an EMT pressing something onto his face.

"What happened?" I ask.

"Line drive smacked him right in the head. That's the downside of having an arm like his. Fast pitches come back at you even faster." The security guard shakes his head. "Poor guy."

I never considered a pitch coming back to hit me in the face when I was pitching. Just the thought of it makes me touch my face, to make sure everything's still where it belongs.

Someone from the Bandits dugout runs toward Hector. I squint to read the number on the back of his jersey. Number thirty-four. Brandon.

"Is Hector going to be okay?" I ask the security guard because there's nobody else to ask, and he's the kind of grown-up who's supposed to tell the truth.

"Probably just a broken nose. These things—they happen more often than you'd think. I'd be more concerned about the psychological repercussions. . . ."

Hector's going to be okay. That's what he's saying. Probably. Sort of. Just a broken nose, maybe.

Hector sits up, carefully. He raises his hand to the sky. *Is there something up there in the clouds?* Not that I can see. He touches his hand lightly to his chest and waves to the sky again. The EMT helps put him on the stretcher and takes him over to an ambulance that's pulled up along the side of the field. The crowd cheers for him.

I cheer, too, but I can't help biting my lip and thinking about what the security guard said. "Psychological repercussions." What the heck are those?

After the game, it's Dad who picks up me and Casey in his truck.

"Can we stop by the hospital?" I ask him once we get buckled in.

"The hospital?" Dad turns down the radio.

"Hector was pitching, and he got hit in the face—"

Casey talks right over me. "The ambulance came to take him away and everything. He was still conscious, but, man, that must have hurt like . . . I don't even know what."

"I'm not sure if they'll let you in to see him, kiddo." Dad taps his fingers on the wheel, waiting for the car in front of us to move.

"But the whole team's going. I asked Brandon and everything. He said we could go," Casey says.

"Come on, Dad. Please? Can we at least try to see him?" Dad from last summer would take us. He always caved when it was me doing the asking.

"Please, Mr. D," Casey pipes in.

"All right, all right." Dad puts on the blinker and heads toward the hospital.

Hector's room isn't hard to find. A bunch of Bandits beat us here. They're standing in the hallway outside his room, laughing about something. I glare at them, but I'm not sure they notice. You don't laugh in the hospital.

Casey runs over to say hi to Brandon and introduce himself to some of the players. He's asking them a zillion questions, like it's no big deal that Hector's in there, in pain, and far away from his family.

I stand quietly against the wall and close my eyes, trying to make the bright lights and the pale green walls disappear. But closing my eyes doesn't make that stuffy chemical smell go away.

Dad stands next to me, but it's almost like he's not even here. Dad from last summer would come up with some silly game to help pass the time, something to distract me from the fact that we're in a hospital, which is a sad and scary place most of the time. But Dad from this summer is so quiet that even I don't know what to say to him. I wonder if he's scared, too.

"Hey, Quinnen, you coming?" Casey is over by

Hector's door with Brandon, about to go in. I snap out of it and follow them.

"Dad?" I say over my shoulder.

"It's okay, Quinnen. I'll keep holding up the wall out here." He laughs at himself, but it seems fake.

When I get in the room, I find Hector propped up in the bed, drinking something out of a white cup with a straw. "Hey," I say.

He smiles at me. There's a bandage on the side of his face. The area is a little puffy, and it's already starting to bruise. That security guard back at the stadium didn't know what he was talking about—Hector's nose looks perfectly fine.

"How are you feeling, man?" Brandon asks.

"Not so great."

"Yeah, I bet."

"Do you want anything from the vending machine?" Casey asks. "Like some chips or cookies or some candy?"

"No, no. I'm not hungry," Hector says.

The TV across from Hector is on ESPN, and it's showing the top baseball plays of the day. We all watch the countdown to the best play: a ridiculous somersault catch by an outfielder for the Oakland Athletics. Casey whispers something to Brandon.

"Me and Case are gonna hop down to the cafeteria for a snack. You okay hanging out with Hector for a bit?" Brandon asks me.

"Sure," I say. Casey almost runs over Brandon getting out of the room. I guess I'd be pretty hungry, too, if I wasn't allowed to eat gluten.

I walk closer to Hector's bed, and he turns down the TV volume. "Does it hurt?" I ask, pointing at the bandage on his face. "Will it leave a scar?"

He puts his drink down on the tray and reaches up to touch the spot lightly with his right hand. "Only a small scar. I have a bigger scar, here." He rolls up his sleeve and turns his right arm over. On the inside of the elbow there's a long scar, maybe half the length of a ruler. It's shiny and lighter than the rest of his skin.

"What happened?"

"*Mi madre*, she turned her back when she was cooking. I was only five, and I reached for the handle of a pan on the stove and pulled it down. The whole thing crashed against my arm and scalded me."

"Ouch! That must've really hurt. Did you have to go to the hospital?"

He shakes his head. "No. The hospital's far away."

When Casey was little, he burned himself on an iron his dad had left on after ironing dress shirts. It didn't even scar, but Mr. Sanders felt so bad about it that he bought Casey a Power Wheel to make up for it.

"I have one, too." I lift up my knee to show him my little half-moon scar. "It's sort of faded now. My mom had me put this ointment on it every day for months so it wouldn't be ugly forever."

"How'd you get it?"

"Me and my sister, Haley, we were biking a few summers ago in the Adirondacks. We go for two weeks every summer because my aunt Julie and uncle Dave have a house there and we can stay for free. Anyway, me and Haley, we were biking over a hill and we were on the right side, but this huge mountain-bike guy came up on the wrong side and crashed into me. I flew over the handlebars and landed real hard on my knee."

"Ouch."

"The guy was really mad at me, too. He said I ran into *him*. He was wearing sandals, so of course his toe got all cut up from the crash. It was nasty. But Haley was having none of it. She called him a big bully and told him he needed to look where he was going. She said you're always supposed to slow down at the top of a hill and didn't he know that? And what if something really bad had happened to me when she was in charge? She told him real good."

I can still see it. Haley in her bike helmet and that shirt she wore all the time that vacation because it had the name of her new favorite band. We rode our bikes together every day. Before boys, before Haley was too cool to ride bikes with me.

"Your sister, I don't remember seeing her at your house."

"She passed away."

Hector's face looks blank. He doesn't understand. Those words must not mean the same thing in Spanish.

"She died," I say. "Last summer."

"I'm sorry. Was she sick?"

I shake my head.

"Do you have another sister or a brother?"

"No," I say. "Only Haley. Do you have any brothers or sisters?"

"I have an older brother, Victor, and a little sister, Mikerline." He grabs his phone from the side table and shows me a picture of him with his brother and sister. His brother is tall and strong-looking—he's probably only a little bit older than Hector—but his sister looks like she's about my age. She has cool braids in her hair and a gap between her front teeth.

"Your family looks nice." I hand the phone back to him. "A brother and a sister. I bet your house is never quiet."

"We have chickens, too."

"Chickens? In your house?"

Hector nods. "*Sí*. My house is very loud."

"My sister, she wasn't quiet. Haley was always playing music or talking with her friends. Or arguing with Mom and Dad." I miss that. Even the arguing. I stare down at the faded scar on my knee.

"But now you've got Brandon staying with you. That must help with the quiet, right?"

Hector's right. My house is less quiet with Brandon. But less quiet doesn't equal less lonely.

"Sort of," I say.

"You have a bigger scar here," Hector says, lightly touching his chest with his hand. He takes another sip from his white cup.

We watch the TV as they show a home run sailing just past the reach of an outfielder's glove.

8

{last summer}

The whole ride back from my game, Haley talked, talked, talked with Zack. About music. About books. About the kids from their camp. And all these inside jokes, too. It was like I wasn't even in the car. And worse, it felt like she was doing it on purpose.

When we were still in Zack's driveway after dropping him off, Haley turned to me. "Do you want to move up to the front seat?"

I wasn't going to sit next to someone who had missed my big hit and then pretended it was no big deal.

"No." I didn't think such a small word could sound so mean, but coming out of my mouth right then, it did.

"Fine," Haley said, backing out of Zack's driveway.

"Suit yourself." She turned up the music—some dumb playlist that Zack had made for her—and for the rest of the ride home, she didn't say anything else to me. I picked at my glove and stared out the window.

When we got home, Haley went out to the back porch and I went straight up to my room. Through the open window, I could hear her downstairs, talking on the phone to one of her friends. Ever since Mom upgraded her cell phone plan at the beginning of the summer, it seemed like all she did was talk to her friends. I had friends, too, but I didn't need to talk to them all day long on the phone. *I* had time for my family, too.

I changed out of my Panthers uniform and into shorts and my favorite Bandits T-shirt and went downstairs to the kitchen to get a Popsicle. Haley was still outside yammering on the phone. *Does her new phone have some kind of super battery that lasts forever?* I wondered.

I took the Popsicle upstairs and slurped it, sitting on my bed. I'd never gotten around to making my bed, and the sheets were all rumpled, sort of like a nest. My nest. As I sucked on the Popsicle, I started thinking about this thing Dad always said when he was talking about a client who was hard to please. "If you can't beat 'em, join 'em." At least, I think that's what he said.

Brain freeze took over, and I gnawed on the Popsicle stick. I guessed I could've eaten it a little slower.

Maybe being anti-Zack wasn't really helping things at all. I knew that when Haley and Mom were fighting, it never helped when Mom tried to tell Haley what not to do. It just made Haley want to do it more.

It was like they were two different teams. Team Mom versus Team Haley. And, as everyone knows, only one team can ever win in a two-team battle.

What if I try to join Haley's team? I wondered. *What's the worst thing that could happen?*

I took the Popsicle stick downstairs and threw it in the kitchen trash.

Haley was finally off the phone and sitting on the living room couch with the TV on.

I sat down on the leather chair next to the couch. "What are you watching?"

"So *now* you're going to talk to me?" Haley didn't even sound like herself anymore. She sounded like one of the mean girls on an MTV show.

I took in a deep breath. *If you can't beat 'em, join 'em.* "Yup."

The commercial ended, and the reality show Haley had been watching came back on. The contestants were supposed to make a dress out of stuff you find in a hardware store. I wouldn't know where to start, and that was before the host of the show said they weren't supposed to use things like tablecloths. It looked impossible.

Haley's phone buzzed. She pulled it out of her pocket and laughed as she read a text message.

"Who is it?" I asked.

"None of your business." Her fingers flew across the little keyboard on her phone. If there was a class in texting, Haley would get an A++.

It was as if I wasn't in the room with her—not really—even though I was only five feet away. I wasn't in the backseat anymore, but still I was invisible.

Used to be that Haley and I would hang out in the living room with the TV on. We'd totally plan on watching something, but then Haley would start telling me about some crazy thing that had happened in her math class or how she'd accidentally hit the gym teacher during volleyball, and then I'd tell her about our basketball game at recess or how Mrs. McCurdy'd had a piece of toilet paper stuck to her shoe for all of social studies, and then, before we knew it, the TV show was over and we'd missed the whole thing.

The TV show was just the background for us, the real deal, the Haley and Quinnen show.

But now it wasn't only the TV that had faded into the background. It was me, too.

By the time they got to the runway part at the end of the episode, I wasn't sure if Haley even cared who was going to win or if she'd bothered to look up from her phone enough to know any of the contestants' names.

The people who made this show sure knew how to ramp up suspense. Right after the runway, they cut to commercial before showing who was going to win the challenge.

During a toothpaste commercial, I decided to try again. "Hey, Haley?"

"Yeah?" She slid her phone back into her pocket. *Finally.*

When she turned her head toward me, I remembered that spot on her neck and how she couldn't answer me on the way to the game about if Zack was her boyfriend or not. "Is Zack . . . is he your boyfriend now?"

"You sound like Mom," Haley said with a little snort. *Ouch.*

I was still waiting for an answer.

She reached up to scratch the spot on her neck. "I don't know, Quinnen. You'd think that's an easy question to answer, but it's not. I like Zack and he likes me, but . . ."

"But what?" I didn't understand how it could be so complicated.

"It's not easy to talk about these things."

"With Zack? But you talk to Zack all the time! Like every day. And you text him all the time, too." Why couldn't she just ask him if he was her boyfriend or not? It was a simple yes-or-no question, right?

"Quinnen, you just don't get it."

"Don't get *what*?" I said. The commercials had ended. The show was back on. But I didn't care who won the challenge anymore. All I wanted was an answer from Haley, a real answer from my sister. The kind I always used to get.

"He's from another town. There are other people he knows who . . . who I don't even know about. His world is totally new to me. It's complicated." Her voice was getting high and she looked a little—almost like she was going to cry.

Other people, I thought. "Other girls?"

"Forget it." Haley bit her lower lip and turned up the TV volume. "You'll never understand."

But I did. At least, I thought I understood. Zack made her sad and angry, but sometimes happy, too. Maybe it was Haley who didn't understand.

Haley had guy friends, and she'd had sort of a boyfriend at school last year, Jacob, but it was different. Jacob had never come over for dinner at our house. And he didn't call Haley all of the time, either. Only some of the time. Plus I knew Jacob. He was on the math team, and his younger brother Ben was in my grade.

But I didn't know Zack. And right then it felt like Haley didn't, either.

I knew that when the show ended she wasn't going to answer my question.

We weren't going to be on the same team. There was no way I could be on Team Haley and Zack. No way.

I could tell that already.

Not this summer.

* * *

"Baaaatter up!" Dad shouted from behind me.

I stepped up to the plate and tried to focus on the pitching machine in front of me, the one that'd be shooting out balls any second. After dinner, Dad had offered to take me to the batting cages. Mom and Haley stayed behind at the house, which was fine. The last thing I wanted was Haley tagging along.

Shwoop. The ball came shooting out. I swung hard, the bat ringing in my hands as the ball shot back. A single, at least. Maybe a double?

"Nice one," Dad said.

"Thanks." I choked up on the bat, gearing up for the next pitch.

Ping!

"It's out of the park! There's some serious lift on that thing! It's *still* going! Oh man, it just blew through a cloud. And did it . . . ? Oh man, it did! Yiiikes. Well, what's one less seagull, anyway? This is one for the record books, folks!"

"Dad!" I was laughing so hard I missed the next two pitches completely.

"Sorry, Quinnbear. I couldn't resist."

Dad managed to keep his fake announcing under control for the next fifteen minutes so I could get in some real hitting practice. I let him hop into the batting cage for the last few minutes so he could hit, too.

It wasn't until we were in the truck headed home

that the sinking feeling came back. I wished we could've stayed in the batting cages all night. Just me and my dad.

"Haley said you had a pretty key hit in the game today," Dad said. "I wish Mom and I could've been there for it. Next summer, I swear, kiddo. Next summer, this client will be history, and I'll have more time to spend with you and your sister."

I stared out the window at the sun, which was finally setting.

"Quinnen?"

"She wasn't even there for it."

"What do you mean?"

Tears crept into my eyes. I blinked hard and fast. Focused on picking at some falling-off foam inside my batting helmet. "She wasn't watching when it happened. She and Zack . . ." I didn't know what I was supposed to tell Dad and not supposed to tell him.

"She was in the bathroom," I finally said. Even though I knew it was a lie. "She missed my hit." My *game-winning* hit.

"I'm sure she felt really bad about missing it, kiddo."

He reached over to pat my shoulder.

"Yeah." I stared at the little pile of gray foam in my batting helmet. "Right."

9

{this summer}

"Quinnen! Hurry up and decide! We're next!" Casey can barely stand still at the ice cream counter. Mom picked us up after the Bandits game—Hector's first game since he got hit in the face—and said me and Casey could go anywhere in town we wanted for a treat. So of course we chose Gracie's. So far this summer, I've barely come here. Just one time with Dad, when we got cones from the takeout window.

Dinner at the ballpark was just a few hours ago, but Casey's jumping up and down and scooting past the people in front of us for a better view of the flavor list. Sixty homemade flavors.

"Hurry it up, Quinnen," Mom says. "There are other people waiting, too."

Dad never rushes me at Gracie's, but I don't tell that to Mom.

I look up at the list. Cookie dough? Mint chocolate chip? None of my favorite flavors look that good tonight, but the lady in front of me is done ordering, and now it's my turn.

"Quinnen! I haven't seen you in so long. What do you want?" It's Haley's friend, Larissa.

"Medium mint chocolate chip in a bowl. Hey, you look different." I stare at her, trying to detect what's changed.

She smiles real wide. "You can't tell? I got my braces off!"

"Right." Her teeth are super-straight and white.

"How are you doing? I've missed seeing you guys." She adds another huge green scoop to my bowl.

"Did you know we're hosting this summer? We got Brandon."

"Sprinkles? They're on me."

"Okay, sure."

She spoons a heap of colored sprinkles onto my ice cream. "Brandon? No way! Can I come over? Help you with your homework? I'm dying to meet him. He's so cute. And, like, a good pitcher, too, right? You must love having him around. I bet he's giving you all kinds of pitching tips."

"Tons," I lie.

"Haley always loved going to Bandits games with

you." Larissa hands me my ice cream cup. She gives me a little smile, but this time her mouth is closed, and I know she must be thinking the same thing as me. How it isn't fair that the one summer we finally get a Bandits player is the summer that Haley's gone.

Larissa starts talking to Casey and Mom about their orders, so I head back to find us a booth. It's always crowded here after games. All the tables are full of families—parents and kids all wearing Bandits T-shirts and caps. I hang out along the wall, waiting for the family in front of me to finish clearing their table. I sit down and mix in the sprinkles with my spoon.

Sometimes it feels wrong even to have a cup of ice cream, knowing that Haley can't.

Back at the counter, Larissa isn't smiling as much now that she's talking to Mom. Mom liked Larissa the best out of Haley's friends. I wonder if she ever wishes Larissa was her other daughter, instead of me.

Casey comes running over with a cone that's almost as big as his face.

"What'd you get?" I ask.

"One scoop of Rocky Road, one scoop of Almond Joy, and one scoop of Mudslide," he says before furiously licking the melted ice cream that's dripping down the side of the cone. I don't ask him if there's gluten in ice cream.

"Do you want a bite?" he asks.

"No thanks," I say. "It's kind of slobbery."

Casey gets pretty quiet and focused on his ice cream.

Out of nowhere, all the girls behind the counter start clapping and cheering. I turn to look at what they see. A bunch of the Bandits are streaming into Gracie's, one after another.

"From the way you guys sounded in the car, I didn't think they had won," Mom says, sitting down with her frozen yogurt cone. "Quinnen never tells me much about the Bandits," she says to Casey, like I'm not even here.

"You don't ask," I whisper.

Mom gives me a funny look but doesn't say anything. She turns to listen to Casey.

"Hector had a bad game," Casey says. "The Bandits had to score eight runs to win. But they did. The catcher hit a grand slam. It was the coolest thing ever." He bites into the Almond Joy scoop and keeps talking with ice cream in his mouth. "At the end, all the guys ran out and jumped on top of each other. It was awesome."

It wasn't awesome for Hector, I think.

Brandon waves at us from his spot in line, and I wave back. I scan all the guys, looking for Hector. He's not there.

I leave my ice cream behind on the table and run over to Brandon.

"Where's Hector?" I ask.

"He's not so happy with himself right now," Brandon says. "We tried to get him to come with us, but he said he couldn't. He said he let the team down." He shrugs. "Hector's got to get over that diva attitude. It's about how the team does. You can't be on your A game every day."

"Easy for you to say."

Brandon would win every game he pitched, even if the Bandits only scored one run each time. It's hard for me to admit it, but he's that good. Best pitching record on the team. Best ERA, too.

"It's his first start in three weeks," Brandon says. "He probably had some nerves. He'll be fine once he gets over himself."

When I return to our table, Casey is almost done filling Mom in on Hector's meltdown—how he walked five batters in four innings and gave up two home runs. I mix my ice cream around with my spoon until it's more soup than ice cream.

"You gonna eat that or drink it?" Casey asks, peeking into my bowl.

I take a little slurp from it, and Mom shakes her head.

We're heading back out to Mom's car when I see someone wearing a Bandits jersey across the street at the playground. Number fifteen. "I'll be right back," I tell Mom and Casey, and jog over.

Hector's facing away from me, sitting on a swing.

I don't want to scare him. It's pretty dark in the

park, except for right under the streetlamps at the edge of the playground.

"Hector?"

He kicks at the wood chips under his feet. He's way too big for the swing. Even with his legs bent all the way, both feet are touching the ground.

I sit down on the swing next to him. Even my feet drag on the ground. Have I really grown that much?

"Do you want to talk?" I ask.

He sniffs. I don't look at his face to see if he's crying or if he just has allergies. It doesn't seem right. "I want to pitch good."

It's well, I think. *You want to pitch* well. But the last thing Hector needs right now is a grammar lesson, so I zip it.

"You will," I say. "That was only one game."

"No. Two games. Two times I failed. Two times I pitched bad." He kicks at the dirt again.

"No one's counting that first game. What happened that day, it wasn't your fault." A breeze comes over the park. I shiver and wish I had my sweatshirt.

"This game, though? This game *was* my fault."

"But you guys won. You won anyway. That's what teammates do. They help each other out."

I think about the Panthers. How last summer it was all of us around the table at Gracie's.

That's what we did to win, too. We always helped each other out.

"I've disappointed my family. My family needs this.

My brother, Victor, he used to play baseball for the Pirates. But he wasn't good enough. They kicked him off the team."

I hold on tight to the chain, turn my head, and listen.

"All Victor wanted his whole life was to play baseball. That was his dream, you know? After they cut him, he had to move to New York City and start a whole new life without baseball. My mother, she expects . . . she expects big things from me. I want to give my family a big house and a car. I want to give my mother everything she wants, everything she deserves. To do that, I need to be good. No—I need to be great."

"But they know you got hurt, right?" I think about what Brandon said back at Gracie's. Of course Hector was nervous being up on the mound for the first time after what had happened. Nerves happen sometimes, even to the very best players.

Hector doesn't answer me.

"You didn't tell them?"

"I didn't want them to worry."

"What about your sister, Mikerline? Did you tell her?"

He swings slightly. He doesn't answer that question, either. "You used to play baseball, right? Did you love it?"

The feeling of the packed dirt of the mound beneath my feet. The butterflies in my belly when I had to pitch to a really good hitter. High-fiving all my friends on the team. The crack of the bat when I sent the ball soaring, soaring, soaring over an outfielder's glove. The post-win ice cream trips with Coach Napoli and his super-long beard. Did I love baseball?

I swallow hard and nod. Of course I did.

"Why did you quit?" Hector asks.

I pick at a bumpy piece of the metal chain. I don't know where to start. "I let them down—my team. I made this big mistake and then . . ."

"What if this is how I'm going to pitch from now on? What if my best days are already behind me? Maybe I should just quit now while I'm ahead." He stares down at the ground as he says it. I can't tell if he's kidding or not. Quitting when he's made it this far?

"Quit? No—you're crazy—what are you talking about?"

"I pitched badly. Don't lie, Quinnen. Today, I was throwing everywhere but the strike zone. I walked three batters *in a row*. Do you know what my ERA is right now? 27.00. *27.00!* I've had bad games before, but I've never seen a stat line like that. Not with my name next to it."

I remember what I told Casey when we were watching from the stands, what I noticed. It's the kind of thing I'm sure the manager noticed, too, but maybe he didn't have a chance to talk to Hector about it yet. "You slowed down a lot between pitches. Starting with the second inning today. In the first inning, you didn't wait long at all before throwing the next pitch. But after that, you did. Like you were overthinking it. You lost your rhythm."

"My rhythm, huh?" He says it slowly. "You're pretty smart about baseball."

I used to be.

"Thanks," I say.

A horn honks, and I turn and see Mom and Casey waving at me. They're waiting for me. But I don't hop off the swing. Not just yet.

I can't let Hector quit. I can't let him give up on himself, let one bad game stop him from doing the thing he loves. "I have an idea," I say. "What if when I came to your games, I yelled something out? To let you know when you're slowing down too much."

Hector stares off into the distance, thinking over what I've just said. "My sister, Mikerline, she always sat in the same seat behind home plate, where I could see her. Maybe she was my good-luck charm. Could you sit in that seat?"

"Of course." I don't tell Hector he's being ridiculously superstitious. He's a baseball player, after all. That would be like telling a cat it's furry. "We'd need some kind of code word for me to yell. Not something obvious; we don't want the other team to know. What could I say?"

Hector doesn't stop to think about it. *"Mofongo."*

"Ma-what, now?"

"*Mofongo*. My favorite food. You don't know *mo-fongo*?"

I shake my head. "I haven't seen it on a menu before. I'll have to try some." I try to say the word again. "*Mo-fongo*." I don't even know how to spell it.

Mom honks the horn longer this time and flicks the car lights. I slide off the swing.

"Wait," Hector says. "You're too nice to do this for me. I should do something for you. Do you want my tickets? To come for free?"

I shake my head. I love the Bandits—I always will—but I'm sick of only watching from the sidelines. If I ever want to be a Panther again, I need to be good, really good. Larissa had the right idea, but she had the wrong person. Brandon would never understand what happened last summer. He couldn't help me. But maybe Hector could.

I cup my hand like I'm holding an invisible base-ball. "Would you . . . could you help me pitch again? I haven't practiced in such a long time."

"Sure," Hector says. "Do you want to practice at the stadium?"

I don't know if Zack is there before the games or not, but I don't want to take any chances. I shake my head. "How about at the park? I bet Brandon can give me a ride."

"Deal," he says.

I stick out my hand to shake on it. "Deal."

As I walk back toward Mom and Casey in the car, I whisper it again and again. *"Mofongo. Mofongo. Mofongo."* I wonder if it's like a hamburger or chicken fingers. *Mofongo* sounds sort of like *fungi*, like mushrooms. There'd better not be any mushrooms in it, because then I'll never want to eat it. I'll have to look it up on the computer when I get home, if I can ever figure out how to spell it.

I know I'm super-full of ice cream—never mind all the junk food I ate at the Bandits game—but for the first time in a while, I feel the littlest bit lighter.

10

{last summer}

"Come on, QD! Strike 'em out!" Mr. Miller yelled from the sidelines. We were one out away from advancing to the regional tournament in Indiana. Only one out away. And I was on the mound.

I felt the stitching on the ball with my pointer finger. *One more strike, Quinnen. One more,* I told myself. I wound up and threw. The batter, the only girl on the opposing team, held her ground. She didn't swing. She knew it was outside, barely.

"Ball two," the umpire said.

"Turds," I muttered under my breath. The score was 2–1, Panthers, with nobody on base, but all it would take was one really good swing from this girl, and the score would be tied.

Nope. Not going to happen, I thought. *Not on my watch.* I stared her down and wound up again. She swung. Swung and hit it. A little dribbler down the first-base line. Easy out. But Damien bobbled it somehow. He bobbled it, and she was safe. Safe at first. *No, no, no!*

"Shake it off, Quinnen!" Coach yelled from the sidelines. I really, really, really couldn't let the next batter get a hit. I had to stop this now.

I took a deep breath. *You've got this; you've got this*, I told myself. I let my breath out. *Okay. I do. I can do this.* I let one fly.

The batter swung. The ball went up, up, up, straight up. Katie flung her helmet off and jogged backward. Our entire team watched as the ball landed in Katie's glove with a little *thunk*. I'm sure the umpire said something about us advancing to the tournament in Indiana, but none of us were listening. We were all running to Katie, high-fiving all over the place. Good thing she was wearing all that padding; otherwise, she would've been covered in bruises.

Katie squealed when I got to her, my raised hands up for double high fives. "We did it!" she screamed, hugging me.

"Watch out, Indiana!" I said.

"You did great, kiddo." Coach patted me on the back. It was hard to tell under all that beard, but I'm pretty sure he was smiling.

"Thanks."

"I think a win this special calls for an extra-special treat. Who's down for some pizza at Antonio's?" Coach asked.

People all the way in Indiana could probably hear us screaming.

Casey's mom came over and squeezed my shoulders extra-hard. "Geez, Mrs. Sanders. Watch out for my arm," I said, laughing.

"Wouldn't want to mess with that," she said. "Your mom and dad must be awfully proud of you."

Well . . . maybe, I thought. I knew Dad was, but sometimes I wasn't so sure about Mom. Sure, she'd come to my games and cheer, but it never felt like she cheered as loud as Dad and Haley. I wondered if she wished I was in the drama club or on the math team instead, like her when she was my age.

"They're coming to the tournament, right?"

I nodded.

When we first realized we'd be going to Indiana if we won this game, Mom and Dad scheduled the time off from work. They wanted to make sure they would be there for my really important games. But what if we hadn't won today and were eliminated?

As I learned when Haley disappeared on me, you never know when you're going to have a big moment until it's happening.

"Let us know if you need a ride to Antonio's," Mrs. Sanders said.

"I will."

I checked my phone to see if Haley had called or sent me a text message during the game. She had special plans for her friend Gretchen's birthday today, but she was going to come pick me up afterward since Mom was working and Dad had an out-of-town meeting. Haley told me she felt bad about missing my game but that it wasn't up to her when Gretchen scheduled her birthday bash. I guessed that was true.

No missed calls. No new text messages.

By the time I had taken off my cleats, put on my flip-flops, and gathered up all my stuff, half the team had already left with their families.

"Is Haley coming to get you?" Katie asked. She chewed on the plastic straw of her water bottle.

I glanced out at the parking lot, expecting to see her car pull in. "Yeah. She should be here any minute."

"Do you want us to wait with you until she gets here?"

I shook my head. "No, that's okay." I checked my phone again.

"See you at Antonio's," Katie said. "I'll save you a seat." As she followed her parents off the field, I carried my bag over to the edge of the parking lot and sat down on the bench. It was bad enough that Mom or Dad couldn't pick me up like all the other parents, but now Haley had to be late, too? And where was Gretchen having her party, anyway? I didn't remember Haley telling me.

Cars pulled out of the parking lot one by one. I dialed Haley's number and pressed the phone to my ear. It went straight to voicemail. "Haley, everyone's leaving. I'm the only one who hasn't been picked up. Are you coming?"

I held my phone in my lap so I wouldn't miss the call or text back. There was only one car left now. Coach's.

I had the worst feeling in my stomach, like I'd eaten way too much ice cream.

Where are you, Haley? I wondered, folding my legs up against my chest and hugging them tight.

Coach's car door opened and he walked out toward me.

"Your folks running late?"

I shook my head. "My sister," I said. "I called her, but nobody answered."

"Haley usually comes to the games, right? Rainbow chair?"

"Yeah," I said. "She used to."

"Did you try calling your parents?"

I shook my head again. "No. I guess I can try." I dialed Dad's cell phone number. It rang and rang. I was about to leave a message when he picked up.

"Quinnen?"

"Dad? My game's over, but Haley isn't here. She didn't come to pick me up."

"Did you try calling her?"

"Yeah," I said. "But her phone is turned off or something."

Dad's voice got a little higher. "I'm at least an hour away, Quinnen. I'm sure Haley's on her way. Maybe she just got tied up."

"Daddy, Coach has to stay with me until someone picks me up. Everyone's at Antonio's by now." I couldn't hold them in any longer. Tears splashed out onto my cheeks. I turned my head away so Coach wouldn't see me cry. There's no crying in baseball—everybody knows that. I rubbed my fist against my face so Coach would think I was scratching an itch on my nose.

Music blared out the window of a car coming down the road. I didn't have to look up to know who it was. "Never mind," I told Dad. "Haley just got here." I hung up the phone.

Coach patted me on the back. "Don't worry about this. I had a teenage brother, too, when I was your age. See you at Antonio's, kiddo."

Haley hadn't said she'd be bringing all of her friends, but the car was full of them. I dragged my bag over to her car and tossed it in the trunk. I didn't even know which back door to open. It didn't look like there was room in the backseat. Or the front seat.

Haley rolled down her window all the way. The music was so loud I could barely hear her. "Whose lap do you want to sit on?"

I didn't want to sit on anybody's lap. I glanced in

the backseat. Gretchen, Larissa, and some other girl I didn't know took up all the spots. One of the other camp counselors, Heaven, was in the front seat next to Haley.

I opened the door on the side with Larissa. She was always nice to me.

"Hop on," she said. "At least you don't weigh much."

"There's no seat belt," I said once I got settled in on Larissa's lap. I hadn't sat on a lap since I was little and used to sit on my grandma's lap. Larissa was a lot bonier than Grandma.

"We're not going far," Haley said.

"Are you giving everyone a ride home?" I asked, hoping somebody's house was just down the street, so I could sit buckled in on a seat like a normal person. I didn't think Mom would be cool with this seating arrangement.

"I'm taking everyone to the movies," Haley said.

The movies?

"But my whole team is at Antonio's," I said. "I thought we were going to . . ." But there was no point in finishing my sentence. Haley had her blinker on to turn right. Left to Antonio's. Right to go to the movie theater. "Haley, come on."

"Majority rules, Quinnen. If you want to go to the movies, raise your hand."

Everyone but me raised a hand.

"If you want to go to Antonio's . . ." Haley was laughing as she gave the option.

"Just stop, Hales. I'm not going to raise my hand."

"I was just trying to be democratic about the whole thing." She smiled at me in the rearview mirror, but I wasn't buying it.

For the rest of the ride to the movie theater, all I could do was stare out the window as Haley and her friends laughed and laughed about something that had happened at Gretchen's party. They wouldn't even give me the details so I could laugh, too. It was like they wanted it to be an inside joke. Like, even if they explained, I wouldn't get it.

Outside, there was a boy a bit younger than Haley, running down the street with a little brown curly-haired dog on a leash. I kept thinking I'd rather be that dog right now than be in this car with my sister and her friends, with all of them laughing. I'd rather be a dog on a leash.

And I didn't even like dogs.

11

{this summer}

The morning I'm supposed to meet up with Hector to work on pitching, Mom knocks on my bedroom door.

"Yeah?"

"Can I come in?" she asks, already opening the door. I don't know why she bothers asking. She always opens the door anyway.

I'm lying on my bed, holding a baseball in my hand. Mom sits down next to me.

"I was wondering . . . ," she says. "I've always wanted to play tennis."

Okay. I wait for her to explain where I come into this.

"I checked with the rec center, and they still have some spots open for tennis lessons. Is that something you would want to do with me?"

"Tennis?" I sit up so I can see Mom better. She's tapping her fingers on her lap, and it looks like she got a manicure recently. She really wants to play tennis? With me?

"Yes, tennis," she says. "Leila Mahoney and her mom just signed up. I think it would be nice for you to try another sport, since . . ."

That's the other thing we never talk about. How baseball sign-ups came and went last winter. How every time Mom or Dad offered to take me, I shrugged it off.

Every time I'd make up a reason, they'd just do that thing where they'd give each other a look, like I wasn't in the room with them. They let me call the shots. Maybe they shouldn't have.

I overheard them talking about it with Miss Ella after one of my sessions. "These things take time," Miss Ella said to them.

Maybe enough time has passed.

I tuck the baseball behind me so Mom can't see.

"I'm not really friends with Leila," I finally say.

Mom's smile goes away. "That doesn't mean you can't become friends with her. Don't you miss spending time with other girls your age?"

In my head, I see me and Katie Miller jumping on her trampoline. And that one time we snuck outside during a sleepover and blasted her brother Andrew with a squirt gun through the open window. His pajama pants were so soaked it looked like he'd wet the bed. And then Katie and I were laughing so hard *we* almost wet our pants.

"No," I say.

"Quinnen . . ."

I shake my head. Tennis players always wear all white and look so clean and preppy. "Can you really see me playing tennis?" Ever since I was five, I've always done a sport. Baseball in the spring, soccer in the fall, basketball in the winter. I'm not very good at soccer or basketball, but I like being on a team, and Dad likes that I play. But tennis?

Tennis is a Haley kind of sport. And since Mom can't ask Haley to play with her, she's asking me.

"I thought it would be nice if we could find something to do together. Just the two of us." Mom stands up, shaking her head. "But if you don't want to . . ."

"Sorry," I say.

Mom closes the door tightly behind her.

I grab my glove from under the bed. No matter how much I wear it, the leather won't stretch out to fit my bigger hand.

"So why are you meeting up with Hector?" Brandon asks as we drive across town to the park. Dad's been letting him borrow the truck to get around town. Maybe he thinks he can sell it for extra on eBay once Brandon becomes famous.

"I told you, it's a secret." I pretend to zip my lips.

"I bet I can weasel your secret out of Casey," he says, turning at the end of the street.

"No way. Casey doesn't even know. I didn't tell him."

"Wow. Keeping secrets from your boyfriend, huh?"

"Are you crazy? Casey is *not* my boyfriend."

"Right. Sorry. My bad." He's smiling. What does he have to smile about? Brandon is so like Haley in that way: always hassling me about Casey. He never lets go of it, even though he has absolutely no proof.

He pulls into the parking lot at the new park in town. It's got a track, a playground, two ball fields, soccer fields, tennis courts, a basketball court—you name it, it's here.

I spot Hector waiting over on the bench. He even brought a few bats.

Brandon unlocks the door. "Well, you come get me when you're ready to go. I'll be over by the track, getting my workout on." He flexes his biceps. *Good grief.*

I head over to Hector. My too-small glove is on my left hand. It feels weird. And not just because it's too small. It feels like it's been forever since I've had a glove on outside at the park.

Someone must have just mowed the fields. There are all these chopped-up bits of grass around the edges.

"Hey, Hector."

He shields his eyes, even though he's wearing

sunglasses, and waves at me. "You want to throw the ball around a little first?"

"Sure."

We jog into the outfield. Hector runs backward until he's about as far away from me as the distance from third base to home plate. He throws the ball at me—hard and fast—and I reach my glove out for it. The ball smacks into my mitt. *Ouch.* I want to shake my hand, but I don't. I don't want Hector to think he has to ease up with me.

I throw the ball back to him. It comes up short and he has to dive to catch it.

"Sorry!" I shout.

"No te preocupes."

"What?"

"No worries." He throws the ball to me again. This time, it doesn't sting so hard. Or maybe I'm just getting used to it.

Soon we're playing catch, throwing the ball back and forth so many times I lose track. My right shoulder is starting to hurt, but I don't care. It's the good kind of hurt, the kind of hurt I've missed.

After I throw the ball to Hector for what feels like the hundredth time, he jogs back to me. "You ready to pitch?" he asks once he's close.

I look over at the pitcher's mound. Someone must have raked the base paths and dusted off the top of the mound earlier this morning. It's so clean and perfect.

"Okay."

I walk over to my old spot. I'm not wearing my cleats, just my sneakers. But I pretend I'm wearing my cleats. Pretend I'm digging them in the littlest bit. Holding my ground.

Hector crouches down behind home plate, where Katie always squatted.

I grip the ball tight in my hand. *I'm pitching,* I tell myself. *I'm really pitching.* It's been eleven months, almost an entire year.

I release the ball. It bounces in the dirt in front of Hector.

"Not bad," he says, throwing the ball back to me.

Yes, bad, I hear. The voice comes from somewhere deep inside me. I heard that voice last summer. Believed that voice when it told me: *This is your chance, Quinnen. Do it now.* That stupid, stupid voice.

I'm trying to tell that voice to can it when I hear another voice—no, *voices.* People laughing.

The sound comes from over by the parking lot. And there's more. Bats clinking against each other. Baseballs thumping in gloves. Someone popping bubble gum. I turn back to see who it is.

The Panthers. At least, some of them. Katie Miller and Joe and Tommy and a bunch of kids I don't know. New Panthers.

That voice in my head is right. I don't belong here. Not anymore.

With the ball still in my hand, the glove on, I take off, running toward Brandon and the track, running to anywhere that isn't the ball field.

"Quinnen!" Hector yells after me. It doesn't take long for him to catch up with me, by the bleachers around the track. I'm panting, but he's barely out of breath.

"What's wrong?" he asks. "Why'd you run?"

All I can do is shake my head. He would never understand. He would never do what I did.

"Quinnen, it's okay. You can tell me."

They're far away now, but I can still hear them. Hear Coach Napoli yelling out instructions for drills. Hear the balls pinging off the bat. I think I can even hear Katie Miller. Is she the only girl on the team now? Or does she have a new friend who's replaced me? I'm sure she does.

I have to squint to look at Hector. "That's my team," I say. "My old team, the Panthers."

"Panthers." He says it back to me slowly.

Panthers forever. Katie and I wrote it on our arms with a Sharpie last year. Mom didn't think it would ever wash off, but it did. It's long gone from my arm now.

If I practice and practice with Hector, if I can be good enough again, would they take me back? After what I did?

"We can try again. Another day," Hector says.

I slide the ball back into my glove and sit down on

the hot metal bleacher. Hector sits next to me. Neither of us says another word as we watch Brandon jog around the track. Around and around and around.

That night, I'm lying on my back on my bedroom floor, softly tossing a baseball up in the air and catching it with my glove. *Thwump. Thwump. Thwump.* The catching is easy. It's the pitching that's hard.

My radio is tuned in to *After Midnight*, and the volume is turned down low enough so only I can hear it. "This is *After Midnight*, with your host, Marcus Allen Andre. Remember, you can always call in with your requests." A song with a jazzy saxophone starts playing.

There's a knock at my door. It's awfully late for Mom or Dad to be knocking.

When I open the door, I find Brandon on the other side. "Hey, squirt," he says.

That's got to be the grossest thing one person could ever call another person. Unless you're talking water guns, most things that squirt are disgusting.

"I'm busy," I say.

"You are so not busy." Brandon barges into my room holding an unopened sleeve of Oreos. "I thought you might want a cookie or two."

I can't exactly say no to a cookie, even if it's Brandon doing the offering. "Fine."

He rips open the sleeve, hands me the top three

cookies, and heads over to my desk. "Has anyone ever told you you're a slob?" He pushes some of my piles to the side.

"Has anyone ever told you you're a turd?" I say. "Oh, wait!"

Brandon chuckles. "You got me there. I'll get you back for that later. I'm the king of pranks."

With a mouthful of cookie, I say, "Foh freally?"

"The other day, me and José—you know, the shortstop—we put Saran Wrap on the toilet seats in the locker room."

I swallow. "No way!"

"It's hard to do. You gotta get it real smooth, 'cause if they see any ripples, they'll know something's there. It's kind of an art."

"Kind of?"

"I'm not going to lie. It gets them every time."

I don't understand why he's in here. Why he knocked on my door, why he brought cookies, why he's telling me a funny story. He's been living in my house for a little over a month, but the whole time it's been like he couldn't care less about me.

"Did you get in trouble for it?" I ask.

"Well, you see, they don't know it's me and José. It's not like they bring in a detective to find out who did it."

"But then you don't get the credit!"

"Eh, I get enough credit."

I have to laugh. No matter what it is, Brandon always has to be the best at it.

Just then, the song ends. I reach over to turn my radio off, but not before Marcus Allen Andre comes on and announces the show.

"You're listening to *After Midnight?*" Brandon's eyebrows are raised.

"No," I say. "It was set there. It's . . ."

"Dude, it's the radio in your room. Who else listens to it?"

There's no lie that will cover it, so I pop in the last cookie.

"It's okay. I mean . . . actually, my girlfriend listens to that radio show, too."

"She does?"

"Yeah. She likes all those cheesy requests, and something about the announcer's voice helps her sleep when she's stressed out." He pulls his phone out of his pocket, flips through a few things, and holds it out to show me. "That's her—Amy."

I try not to get any chocolate on the phone when I take it from him. On the screen is a picture of Brandon wearing a suit with his arm around a girl. She has long curly black hair and glasses, and she's all dressed up, too. She's pretty, but not the kind of girl I pictured Brandon with. She looks nice. "Where does she live?"

"Her vet school's in Colorado. We met at Stanford. She was on the women's softball team." He takes the phone back from me. "I should probably give her a call. She's got a big test coming up, and she's freaking out."

"Thanks for the cookies," I say as Brandon heads for the door.

"No prob," he says. "You know, you're really lucky that Hector's putting aside the time to help you with pitching. My boy misses his family back in the Dominican like crazy. I think it's helping him feel more comfortable here, hanging out with you. Like you're his substitute little sister or something."

I don't know what to say.

"Well, I gotta go call my girl. Night, Quinnen."

"Night, Brandon."

He closes the door a little too loudly, and when he gets back in his room, he's so loud on the phone with Amy that I can barely hear *After Midnight*.

But that's okay. Tonight, I don't mind.

12

{last summer}

Dad insisted we drive all the way to the Adirondacks in one day, since we had to cut our vacation short by a week to be back in time for a mandatory practice and my baseball tournament. We started driving at five in the morning, and we were only outside Toledo, not even a third of the way there.

"Honey, did I close all the windows?" Mom asked Dad.

"You know, I think you might've left one open. We should probably turn around now. We're only, like, five hours away." Haley snorted after she said it.

"Hales . . . ," Dad said.

"Come on, Mom. You always do this. Remember that time you thought the house was going to burn down because you left the bathroom fan on? It didn't. What's the worst that can happen from leaving a window open, anyway?" Haley stared out the car window, shaking her head. I'm not sure she could get farther away from me in the backseat if she tried.

"She has a point, dear." Dad yawned.

"But what if it was open wide enough that a skunk crawled through and turned the house into its own stinky home?" I asked.

"I guess then the rest of the house would smell like your room," Haley said.

"My room doesn't smell like skunk!"

"You're so used to it you can't even tell anymore."

"Girls, that's enough," Mom said. "Please."

"At least it doesn't smell like nail polish," I said. Haley had had all her friends over to paint their nails the day before, and the house still smelled like stinky nail polish when we left. I hoped Mom *had* left the window open. Maybe then it wouldn't stink when we got back.

"You're just mad because you weren't invited," Haley said.

"Am not." I pulled a book out of my backpack. It was called *Savvy*, and it was on my summer reading list. The real one, not Haley's. After missing out on Antonio's with my teammates, I'd thrown Haley's list in the recycling. The librarian posted the books we were actually supposed to read online, anyway.

Reading in the car always made me a little sick to my stomach, but it was a whole lot better than talking to my sister.

Haley took out her cell phone. Time to give Zack or one of her friends another update.

I didn't know why I cared what she was doing. I had a life. I had my own stuff going on.

Maybe I would find out I had a special power, like Mibs in my book. There was still another month left of summer. Plenty of time to discover that I could fly or be invisible. Or turn back time.

When we pulled up to Aunt Julie and Uncle Dave's house, it was almost midnight. Mom had fallen asleep, but Dad, Haley, and I were wide-awake, thanks to Mountain Dew.

I shivered when I stepped out of the car. It was a lot cooler in the mountains than it was back home, and I couldn't see much because there were all these trees trapping us in. They looked like gigantic Christmas trees, and it smelled like Christmas, too.

Dad put his hand on my shoulder. "Check under the mat for the key. You do the honors."

I ran up the steps and felt under the woven doormat for the key. I found it and put it in the lock. It was a little sticky, but I turned it with all my strength until I heard a click.

The door opened with a creak. The trees blocked the moonlight from reaching us, making it extra-dark. I flipped on the light switch and went from room to room downstairs, turning on all the lights.

Everything was in its right place from last summer and the summer before that. We'd been coming here every summer since I was four. There was the weird monkey lamp, right where it belonged on the table next to the faded yellow sofa. And the bookcase filled with board games that we would play late into the night because nobody had to go to work or school the next day.

While Dad and Haley started bringing in our suitcases and the bags of food Mom had packed, I raced upstairs to turn on more lights. The upstairs was a little creepy, so I always turned the lights on at night, even if we were all downstairs.

I turned on the upstairs hall light, then the light in the master bedroom. I still didn't know why they called it that; Dad and Mom weren't the masters of anything. The next room was the bathroom, with a tub that sat right in the middle of the floor and had weird brass clawed feet on it. Then my and Haley's room, with the old leather chair that was perfect for reading on a rainy day, and the bunk beds, and all the weird old dolls from when Aunt Julie and my mom were little kids. I always turned them around so they wouldn't watch me while I slept.

"I call top bunk!" I yelled downstairs so Haley could hear. We always did dibs for top bunk.

I ran back downstairs to grab my bag, took it upstairs, and started unpacking. I put the clothes Mom had folded into the bureau drawers and waited for Haley to come up. Finally I heard her footsteps on the stairs.

"Haley! Did you hear me? I called top bunk."

She popped her head in the room. "Yeah? Cool. This time, you can have top bunk *and* bottom bunk. You can switch each night."

"Wait, what?"

"I'm going to stay in the nursery."

Last year, Aunt Julie and Uncle Dave turned the tiny office at the end of the hall into a nursery for my little cousin, Chloe. "You're staying in the baby's room?"

"Yeah," Haley said. "They've got the daybed in there. That way I won't keep you up when I'm talking to Zack or my friends." She sounded so cheery, like this was such a great idea.

"But you always stay in this room," I said. "With me."

"Quinnen, I'm sixteen. I need my own space."

I can give you space, I thought.

Haley turned and went into her room—her new room—and I threw the rest of my clothes in the bureau. I didn't care if they were neat and folded anymore. Who was going to see them, except for me? I had the room to myself.

I turned on the little night-light, climbed up to the top bunk, and crawled under the covers. There was a little ledge up here, where I used to put a cool rock or an action figure whenever I had beaten Haley to calling top bunk. Haley always put a book on it when she stayed up here. The springs creaked as I turned over onto my side.

Haley was already on the phone in her room. The walls were so thin I could hear everything she said. "It's okay that you say it. Really, I . . ." She laughed. It was a new laugh. Her Zack laugh. "Okay. It's late. I . . . I love you, too."

I rubbed the sheet in between my fingers and closed my eyes.

I didn't know who my sister was anymore.

13

{this summer}

I look down at my watch. Hector's taken at least two seconds longer between the last couple pitches. He's slowing down. He's thinking too hard.

"Come on! Strike 'em out," the man in front of me yells.

"You got him, Hector!" Casey screams.

"*Mofongo!*"

"Ma-what?" Casey looks at me like I have ten heads and none of them is wearing a Bandits cap.

"It's Spanish," I say. "It's like a good-luck thing, for Hector."

"Can I say it, too?"

I think about our pact. Hector didn't make me pinky-swear I wouldn't tell Casey. But still. It's our thing. I shake my head. "No. He just wanted me to say it. It's hard to explain."

"Just you, huh?" Casey says. He turns back to face the game.

The batter swings and misses. Hector's struck him out. His second strikeout this inning. It's working! Dad would say I nipped it in the bud. Well, if I told him. He and Mom think I've been tagging along with Brandon when he goes to the park. "Yeah, Hector!"

Everyone is clapping and cheering, except for Casey, who's looking at his phone. He never takes his phone out during the game. He knows it drives me crazy.

"Aren't you going to cheer for Hector?" I ask him.

"Yeah," he says. "In a minute."

Whatever, Case. I catch Hector's eye as he heads back into the dugout, and he waves at me.

"He waved at me. Casey, you missed it. He waved!" Casey groans.

After the game, Mrs. Sanders takes me and Casey to the new Mexican restaurant in town. She's all jazzed about their special gluten-free menu. She drops me off at my house afterward. "Thanks for the ride and the burrito!" I tell her as I hop out of the van. I still can't believe that Hector won tonight. He pitched like a pro. Maybe even better than Brandon.

When I walk inside the house, Mom, Dad, and Brandon are all in the living room.

So are Brandon's bags. All four of them.

"Isn't the road trip *next* week?" I ask. But I already know it is. I wrote it on my calendar.

"Brandon's got some exciting news." Dad is smiling, but it's so wide and toothy it looks like he's pretending. "Tell her!"

"The manager called me into his office after the game," Brandon says. "They need me up at Double-A. We're about to head over to O'Hare to see if I can catch the last flight of the day." He keeps nodding as he says each word, like he can't believe it's real.

"But . . ." I finish the rest in my head: *I was finally starting to like you.* "That's . . ." The right word doesn't come immediately. ". . . awesome." I look at Brandon, then at Mom and Dad.

"It's all happening kind of fast, isn't it?" Mom says. "We were just getting used to having you around. We're sure going to miss you." Her eyes are tearing up, even though she never seemed super-attached to Brandon.

"Can I come with you to the airport?" I ask.

"Sure," Dad says. "Come on, let's load 'em up!"

Brandon grabs two of his bags, Dad takes another, and I take the last one out to the truck. Brandon doesn't say a word this time about me not being strong enough. He knows I am. Dad pulls the cover over them once they're all in there, and we get in the cab.

"When are you going to pitch?" I ask Brandon as Dad backs the truck out of the driveway.

"Tomorrow. Can you believe it? I'm so stoked. Some of the guys I'll be pitching to have played in the majors. Did you know that? All that stands between me and the majors now is Triple-A."

"Why did they pick you?"

"Well, I've got the goods, for one. But really, they know I can handle it at this level. I've made five starts and shut 'em down every time. They said they want to see what I can do at Double-A."

I nod.

"Oh, and the guy who was supposed to pitch tomorrow tore something in his shoulder, and they needed someone who had had enough rest."

"So it's you."

"It's me!" Brandon takes his buzzing cell phone out of his pocket. I can only imagine how many texts he's going to get over the next couple hours. "Oh, shoot! I still need to call Amy. And try my parents again."

"Don't worry about us," Dad says. "You make all the calls you need. We won't be at O'Hare for at least an hour."

While Brandon's on the phone, Dad and I don't talk. We don't need to. Brandon is doing enough talking for all three of us. Maybe more. I know I'm not supposed to listen to other people's phone calls—that it's rude—but what else am I supposed to do? Look out the window? Play the license-plate game? It's late at night, and the roads really aren't that busy.

When Brandon calls Amy, he sounds excited about

being just a state away from her. And when he calls his mom, she's flipping out so much I can hear almost every word she's saying. A whole lot of "Oh my good-nesses." I hope she can handle herself when Brandon makes the big leagues. Otherwise, she's going to be one of those parents who can't even sit in the stadium, the kind who have to be outside, pacing back and forth. Brandon's dad comes onto the phone, and now Brandon sounds like he's got something caught in his throat. If I didn't know him better, I'd think he was going to cry.

"Arizona," he says. "Yeah, Pop. Just like in spring training."

I glance at Brandon. He's not crying, but he might have something in his eye.

"Can't wait to see you, too. Love you. Bye." He puts his phone down on his lap. "My parents are booking flights right now. They're gonna be at my game tomor-row."

"I bet they're so proud of you," Dad says.

"They're excited," Brandon says. He can't stop drumming his hands on the door. It would have driven me crazy earlier this summer, but now I don't mind it so much.

For the rest of the ride, the three of us talk about how we think the Bandits are going to do against their next opponent and which Bandit will end up with the highest batting average and the most home runs.

As Dad takes the exit for the airport, I have this

weird feeling in my stomach. It's not butterflies and it's not a stomachache from the burrito. I think people call it déjà vu, except I don't totally know what that means. Still, I'm almost sure that's what it is.

Dad pulls up by the sign for United and puts the truck into park. Brandon hops out. Even though I'm in the middle seat and I'm not leaving, I hop out, too. Dad gets Brandon's bags out of the back for him.

"Hey, Mr. D?"

"Yeah," Dad says, putting the last duffel bag down.

"Thanks for letting me stay with you guys. It was nice having a place to come home to every night that felt like home."

"Anytime," Dad says. "I'm glad we could help."

Brandon crouches down so he's at my level. I brush a piece of hair out of my face so I can look him in the eye.

"I'm gonna miss you, squirt," he says.

"Me too." I swallow hard. "I don't know what the Bandits are gonna do without you."

"They'll be fine," he says. "You keep an eye on Hector for me. I think it helped him out a lot—you being there for him at the game today. He's an ace. You know that, right?"

I nod. And then I don't know what I'm doing because my arms are wrapped around Brandon and he's hugging me back, tight, and lifting me off the ground.

"Well, I'd better get going. If there's one flight I can't miss," Brandon says, "this is it."

"Have a safe trip," Dad says. "Text me to let us know you got in all right."

We both get back in the truck before the airport policewoman gets mad at us for double-parking. Even after I watch Brandon walk through the sliding glass doors and I can't see him anymore, I keep glancing back at the airport. I stare at the terminal in the side mirror until we're too far away and it hurts my neck to do it, and then I close my eyes.

When I open them, we're on the highway. I look up at the sky. We're too close to the city to see the stars. The sky's all orange and yellow and brown. Those aren't sky colors. But as we get closer to home, the sky turns back into that deep shade of blue, and the stars come into view.

"Is someone else going to stay with us, now that Brandon's gone?" I ask Dad.

"I haven't thought that far ahead." He clears his throat. "We'll see."

I hate that answer. It's just a grown-up way of saying no.

It's after midnight by the time we get home, and all I can hear are the crickets and the sound of a train whistle in the distance.

"Hey, kiddo?" Dad finally speaking startles me as we make our way to the front door, the moon lighting the way. "Your mom and I would really like to come to a Bandits game with you. For all of us to go together as a family. How about next week, when Casey's on vacation?"

"The Bandits are on the road. But they'll be back for the weekend."

"How about Saturday, then?"

"I guess." I wish I could tell him that it's not the same. We can't do anything "as a family" anymore. It's not possible. One of us is missing.

I head upstairs while Dad goes into the kitchen.

The door to the room Brandon was staying in is open. I peek inside. Mom has already changed the sheets and made up the bed for guests. There are vacuum marks on the carpet.

It's like he was never here.

I go into my room. At least it always looks like someone lives here. I'm glad Mom hasn't brought her cleaning operation into my bedroom. I change into my pajamas and toss my clothes into the right piles on the floor, but then I notice something out of the corner of my eye.

Two brand-new baseballs on my bookshelf. And a note underneath.

I hop over the piles to get to them.

Something is scribbled on each ball, exactly the same. I think I can make out a B.

I open the note, written on the back of the scratch paper we keep by the computer.

Quinnen,

You didn't think I would forget, did you? I know you need a memento of the time you lived with a baseball player before he was crazy famous and his signature went for thousands on eBay. One's for you, the other for Casey.

Casey told me you used to be a really good pitcher. You know, there's this Japanese knuckleball pitcher who plays pro ball—a girl. I saw her pitch once when she was playing for a team in California. She's tiny—I bet you'll end up taller—but, man, can she throw.

Don't give up too early.

Just saying.

Anyway, you better come watch me when I make it to the majors. I'll leave tickets for you and your parents. Maybe even Casey, if he's lucky.

Bandits forever!

> *Love,*
> *Brandon #34*

I hold one of the balls in my hand and look closely at the signature. *Brandon Williams.* I have an official baseball signed by Brandon Williams. I take it into bed with me, placing it on my left side as I lie down and flip through the new *Sports Illustrated for Kids* that came in the mail. I hear Dad come up the stairs, brush his teeth, and head down the hall to his and Mom's bedroom.

And then all I hear is silence. I don't hear Brandon putting down the toilet seat. He was the loudest of anyone ever, I swear. I don't hear him trying to talk quietly on the phone to Amy or typing on his laptop. And I don't hear him playing Xbox with the volume down real low.

I didn't think I could ever miss someone who wasn't Haley. Didn't think I needed someone in my house who wasn't my sister.

But I do.

I drop my magazine to the floor and walk over to Haley's room. I close the door gently behind me. Nobody comes in here anymore. Or if they do, they don't touch anything. Everything is still the way it used to be. The laundry piled on the edge of her unmade bed. All of her books on the bookshelves. The moon casts a glow over her computer; the screen is coated in dust.

It can't stay this way forever.

I turn on the light and try to see her room the way one of those interior decorators from those HGTV shows that Mom always watches would see it. "Looking for the potential." Haley's room is almost too big for one person. It's at least twice as big as the room Brandon stayed in. You could fit twin beds in here easily and still have room for other furniture.

I turn off the light and head back into my room.

Somewhere in my desk mess is a big pad of drawing paper from art class. There must be some sheets left. I toss aside old math assignments, handouts, and magazines until I find it.

There isn't enough space on my desk, so I clear a spot on the floor and lie down on my belly. I sketch ways to rearrange Haley's room using furniture from the guest room, just like an interior decorator, and then I color it in with some markers.

I draw and draw and draw, not even thinking about how late it is or that I'm supposed to be sleeping. At least it's not quiet anymore. The markers squeak on the page, but in my head there are other sounds. Guys laughing as they come in from a game in their grass-stained uniforms. ESPN on all the time. We could fit three baseball players here each summer, between Haley's old room and the guest bedroom. I'm sure of it.

When I finish, I sit up and look at my drawing. I'm not as good a student as Haley was, but I usually get an A in art.

But now all those sounds are gone and all I can hear are the crickets and the clock in the hallway, and it seems like the thing that I thought would fix everything is actually doing something else. It feels like I just took a big eraser to my sister. To everything that was left of her.

I crumple up the paper and throw it toward the trash can. It misses, and I leave it there.

I grab the ball from Brandon and go into Haley's room. The clock on her nightstand is still blinking from when we lost power in the winter. Nobody came in and reset it. I turn the clock so it faces the wall. I crawl under the covers, even though they don't smell like Haley anymore, and this time I don't tell myself that I can't do it. I tell myself, *It's okay, Quinnen. It's okay.*

And out loud I tell Haley's pillow, "I'm sorry, I'm sorry, I'm sorry."

14

{last summer}

"Oh, Quin-nen . . ." The voice came out in a singsong.

Someone flipped up the shade, and sunlight streamed into the bedroom. It was our third day in the Adirondacks.

"Dad?" I glanced at the travel alarm clock I'd put on the ledge by the top bunk. "It's seven o'clock. That's too early for summer."

"Too early? It's never too early for an adventure."

"What adventure?" I asked. I sat up so fast I whacked my head on the ceiling. "Ouch."

"How does a hike up Old Black Bear sound?" Dad said as he opened the door to the room where Haley was staying.

"Like torture," Haley groaned. "This is supposed to be a vacation."

"Sounds fun," I said, rubbing my head.

Dad popped his head back into my room. "There are doughnuts for breakfast, and Mom is making some lunches to take to the top. You girls just need to get dressed and brush your teeth, and we're all set to go." He headed downstairs.

Haley stumbled out of her bedroom toward the bathroom.

"Maybe we'll see a bear," I said, loud enough for her to hear. I'd always wanted to see one. Not at the zoo—I'd seen plenty at the zoo—but up close. Well, not *too* up close. Close enough that I could take a picture of it with the zoom.

"Yeah," Haley said. "Maybe it'll eat me so I won't have to go on the hike."

"Slow down, Quinnbear," Dad said. "We need to wait for Mom and Haley to catch up." Dad and I were always the fastest on hikes. Mom and Haley usually dawdled.

I pulled off to the side of the trail and grabbed on to a tree while I caught my breath. Dad took a few sips from his water bottle, then handed it to me. I gulped a couple mouthfuls of water and looked down the trail. Hiking up the mountain, one step after another, I had kept my eyes on the ground so I wouldn't trip. Now I could see how high we were. And how far we still had to go.

I was getting sweaty from the climb, so I took off my long-sleeve T-shirt and tied it around my waist. I shivered for a moment in my tank top and moved over to a spot where the sun shone through the leaves.

"Are you starting to get excited for the tournament?" Dad asked.

"Starting?"

"It's a big accomplishment, Quinnen. I hope you know how proud Mom and I are of you."

"I know," I said quietly, staring down at Mom and Haley, who still had a ways to go before catching up with us. I wondered what the two of them were talking about. Was Haley telling Mom all the things about Zack that she wouldn't tell me?

"How long do you think Coach Napoli's beard will be by the time we get back from vacation?" Dad asked, stroking his bare chin.

"Hopefully long enough for him to sit on it. Like wizard-long. Dumbledore-long."

Dad smiled. "Dumbledore, huh? We'll see."

Finally Mom and Haley caught up with us. Dad said we had to give them some time to rest, too, if we were going to be fair.

Haley pulled her cell phone out of the pocket of her shorts.

"Hales, really?" Dad said.

She shoved it back in her pocket. "It's not like we get reception up here, anyway. Onward?"

Mom went up ahead with Dad while I stayed back with Haley.

"How far do you think we'll be able to see when we get to the top?" I asked, keeping my eyes on Haley's sneakers as she took each careful step.

"To outer space."

"Come on."

"I don't know, Quinnen. Can you stop asking so many annoying questions?"

It was only one question. I stayed quiet until something rustled in the grass nearby and we stopped to see what it was. A chipmunk popped its head out, and I yelped.

Haley laughed.

"What?"

"Oh, nothing," she said. "I was just thinking about how this morning you said you wanted to see a bear and now you're freaking out over a chipmunk."

"Am not," I said. But I was laughing, too.

We got quieter as the trail steepened and became rockier, but it was the good kind of quiet, not the fighting kind. Dad and Mom were talking a lot, which slowed them down, so it didn't matter that Haley was poky. We were all kind of poky together there on the side of the mountain, just my family and the chipmunks and the birds.

The wind picked up as we got closer to the top, and it wasn't as warm as it had been back at the house.

The top of the mountain was made up of all these huge jagged rocks. Even Mom and Dad had to climb on their hands and knees.

For once, it helped to be the shortest one. I scrambled past the others up the rocks and ran to the very top. I spun and spun and looked in every direction. Everywhere I looked was blue and green and curvy. So alive. There were tons of other mountains in the distance—so many we'd never have time to climb them all. It was nothing like home.

"It makes you feel pretty small, being up here." Haley came and stood next to me, breathing hard as she looked into the distance. She handed me a Twizzler. "Shh. Mom doesn't know I brought them. They're just for us."

I gobbled mine up real fast, popped a few more in my pocket for later, and went over to where Mom and Dad were sitting. Dad was already pulling the sandwiches out of his backpack. "Don't eat without me!" I yelled.

"One peanut butter and banana sandwich," Dad said, handing it to me. "Was that so torturous?" he asked Haley.

Haley smiled. "Not entirely. I guess you're not Stalin."

Mom and Dad laughed.

"Who's stallin'?" I asked.

They just laughed harder.

"Come on!"

"Look it up when we're back at the house," Mom said.

"You guys are no fun," I said. But I was smiling. I opened up a bag of Fritos and tossed a handful into my mouth. Haley grabbed the bag from me, and then Mom decided she didn't need to eat healthy during vacation and had some, too, and then Dad poured the rest into his mouth like he was Chip Monster.

And Haley didn't check her phone, even though we were at the top of the mountain and she probably had cell reception. Not even once.

When we got back to the house, it was almost time for supper, but Mom said she didn't feel like cooking, so she ordered a pizza. She and Dad drove into town to pick it up, leaving me and Haley at the house.

"I call first bath!" Haley said. She started filling up the tub, went into her bedroom for clean clothes, and closed the bathroom door. I was lying on the bottom bunk, reading the first chapter of this scary Stephen King paperback I had found downstairs. The creepy clown on the cover hadn't come into it yet, but I figured if I kept reading, it would get good.

I could hear Haley's cell phone buzzing on the wooden dresser in her room.

A text message.

I tried to read my book, but I must have read the

same sentence ten times and I couldn't say what it was about. I closed the book, left it on my bed, and went into Haley's room. In the bathroom, she was singing this song we'd heard on the radio in the car. I picked up her phone.

One new text message.

It was from Zack: *Did you survive the hike?*

When I scrolled up, I could see all the messages between Zack and Haley. So many messages. Some were in Spanish, so I couldn't understand them. But there were more. So many more in English, and I read them. All of them. It was like watching Haley and Zack talk, except I wasn't invited. I wasn't supposed to see any of it, but I couldn't stop.

I couldn't stop reading them.

And then I saw it.

Nothing says "family vacation" like a forced march with your annoying sister. At least I have a room to myself this time. There's no way I could've handled a whole week stuck in the same room as her. She's so immature and clingy. Only four days till I get back. Can't come soon enough.

My heart was beating hard, like when I'm up at bat and there are two outs and a 3-2 count and everything comes down to me and my one chance and I can't blow it.

And then I started typing.

I think we should brake up.

And then I hit "Send."

15

{this summer}

"Quinnen! Time to go!" Dad yells up the stairs.

I'm searching under my bed for my Bandits T-shirt. I know it's under there somewhere.

"Coming!" I yell back.

Found it! It passes the sniff test, so I put it on and run down the stairs. Dad is waiting outside by the truck, but Mom is already sitting inside it, tapping her fingers on the dash.

I climb in through Dad's side and sit in the middle.

"I started reading the new book-club book last night," Mom says. She waits for me to say something back. She hasn't bugged me about tennis lessons since that day a few weeks ago, but she won't let go about the stupid mother-daughter book club. Even though we missed the first meeting, where they talked about

142

the Judy Blume book, she still insists we can join in for the second book, *When You Reach Me.*

I stare out the window as we pass by Casey's empty house.

"Quinnen?"

"What, Mom?"

"I'm talking to you."

"I know. You started reading the book. That's not exactly big news. It's not like you didn't already know how to read."

"Quinnen!" Dad raises his voice and glances over my head at Mom. "I don't like your tone."

"What do you want me to say?" I ask him.

"Did you read the book yet?" he asks.

I don't tell them that I read the whole thing. Or that I checked the bookshelf downstairs to see if Haley had any more books by Rebecca Stead. She didn't. Mom always said she and Haley were the bookworms. Never her and me. I know she wouldn't have chosen me for the book club if Haley was still here.

"I read a few pages," I say. "But it's not really my kind of book, you know?"

Mom clasps her hands together on her lap and sighs. "I thought you might like this one. I love the mystery of it."

I shrug.

After a few minutes, I reach over and turn the radio up so we don't have to talk for the rest of the ride to the ballpark.

Mom and Dad couldn't be slower when it comes to walking to the ticket booth. I have to keep reminding myself to walk extra-slow to stay with them, since they have the money for the tickets and food. And because we're doing this "as a family."

At the ticket booth, Mrs. Harrington nearly squeals when she sees my mom. "Laurie! So good to see you here with your family."

"It's nice to be back." Mom hands her the money for our tickets.

"I've been thinking about you folks this summer. So happy to hear you're hosting. Is Brandon's replacement staying with you, too?"

"I'm not sure if we're going to take another one in just yet," Mom says. "It's a lot to get used to someone and then have him leave."

She talks like I'm not standing right here next to her, like I don't have opinions, like I'm not a voting member of the Donnelly family.

"I think we should," I say quietly.

"What's that, dear?" Mrs. Harrington asks.

"I said, I think we should get another one."

Mom shakes her head. "She doesn't . . ."

I don't what?

"There's always next summer," Mrs. Harrington says.

Mom breaks off a ticket, hands it to me, and says something to Dad that I can't hear as we walk into the stadium.

I head straight for our seats right behind home plate. Hector's pitching this afternoon and I want to make sure nobody sneaks into my special spot. Plus I don't want to run into Zack. "Can you bring me back a hot dog?" I ask Dad.

"You want mustard?" he asks.

"Yup."

"How about fries?"

"Sure."

I see Hector warming up his pitching arm with some stretches over by the dugout.

"Hey, Hector!" I shout. He looks over and waves. I wave back.

The visiting team, the Coal Miners, must be eating all the food that Casey isn't allowed to have, because their players are ginormous. And they're smacking every other pitch deep into the outfield. *Uh-oh.* I hope Hector isn't watching.

"I couldn't find you for a second," Dad says. He's carrying a cardboard box full of hot dogs and fries. He glances at the empty seat on either side of me. "There aren't . . ."

But then he stops himself. I know what he was going to say because I still do it, too, sometimes. Look for four in a row—when all we need now is three.

He sits down next to me. "Think they're going to win today?"

I nod. "They're the Bandits, Dad." With Hector on

the mound and me here to help, there's no way the Coal Miners are going to win this one.

Dad laughs.

Mom's so busy chatting with some old co-workers from the community college that she doesn't join us until right before the first pitch. She sits on the other side of me.

"So, do you know much about the pitcher?" Mom asks as Hector takes the mound for the Bandits.

I finish chewing my mouthful of hot dog and fill her in on Hector's strengths: great slider, 95-mile-per-hour fastball, and a nasty curveball. I leave out the part about our secret deal. We only met up two times before Brandon left, and then the Bandits went on the road, so we haven't had a chance to meet up again to work on pitching.

"Hector, is it?" Mom says. "He's the one who . . ." She glances over at Dad for a second. "Never mind." She shakes her head. "You really study up on this stuff, huh?"

"Yup." I keep my eyes glued to the ball as it leaves Hector's hand. The batter makes good contact, and the ball shoots right up the middle, between the second baseman and the shortstop.

"Come on, Bandits! You've got this, Hec. Shake it off!" I stand up so he can really hear me.

The next batter steps into the box. He holds his bat above his head, and he looks ridiculous. Casey would get a kick out of him.

"You've got 'em, Hector!" Mom yells, leaning forward. I almost spit out my root beer. "Am I doing it right?" she asks quietly.

"Cheering? I don't think there's a wrong way."

"Good."

She settles back into her seat for the rest of the inning, but when the Bandits shortstop hits a home run, she stands up and cheers with me and Dad and every other Bandits fan.

When we sit back down, she turns to me. "You know, this is pretty fun."

No kidding, I think. But I don't say that. "Yeah, it is."

"I didn't realize how much I was missing out on every summer by teaching at the community college," Mom says. "It's nice having the extra time with you this summer."

I don't know what to say back to her. The only reason she stopped teaching was because of Haley. It doesn't seem possible, or fair, that anything nice or good should happen because Haley's gone.

"Come on, Hec!" I shout, cupping my hands around my mouth.

He's pitching so well I haven't had to say *mofongo* today. Which is probably a good thing because then I'd have to explain it to Mom and Dad. I'm not ready to tell them that I want to be a Panther again.

In the middle of the fifth inning, Banjo runs out onto the field with a microphone. "I need three volunteers. Who wants to help ol' Banjo out?"

Mom looks at me. "You should do it."

I shake my head. "These things are silly."

"But they're fun. And soon you'll be too old for them. Plus I bet you'll get a prize. Maybe one of those new Bandits sweatshirts they were selling at the store."

Mom's right—you usually don't even have to win the game to get a prize. And a new Bandits sweatshirt would be the perfect thing to wear on the first day of school.

"Okay." I stand up, waving my hand. Banjo raises his hand up over his eyes, like he's searching the high seas, not just looking for contestants for the latest mid-inning game. He doesn't go for the kids at first. He chooses an older man wearing Bandits gear from head to toe and then a teenage girl.

Pick me! Pick me! There's no way he can't see me. I'm waving both hands and jumping. He scans the entire crowd one more time and then points directly at me.

I run down to the gate where they let us onto the field.

Banjo has each of us tell the crowd our name into the microphone.

"Quinnen!" he says, repeating what I said. "What an unuuuusual name!"

I smile back at him like he's the first person to ever tell me my name is unique.

"We're debuting a brand-new game today here at Abbott Memorial Stadium. Pizza Knockout!"

I swallow hard.

Running out from the on-field entrance are three people dressed up as slices of pizza. Pepperoni. Sausage. Cheese.

The person dressed as a slice of cheese pizza is wearing beat-up black Converse sneakers.

Cheese Pizza is Zack.

16

{last summer}

I stared down at Haley's phone, waiting for Zack to write back. I could still hear Haley singing in the bathroom. The time on the clock changed to 6:35 . . . 6:36 . . . 6:37.

Nothing.

I was still holding the phone in the palm of my hand when I heard the front door open.

"Pizza time!" Dad yelled.

I put the phone back on Haley's bureau in the exact same place I had found it and went downstairs.

The pizza box was open on the kitchen counter: half pepperoni for me and Haley, half green peppers and onions for Mom and Dad. It was the way we always got our pizza. Dad was pouring root beer into tall glasses while Mom put plates and napkins at our places.

"Did you tell your sister it's time for dinner?" Mom asked.

"Yeah," I said, even though I hadn't. "She'll be down soon." I grabbed a slice of pepperoni out of the box and put it on my plate.

Dad and Mom sat down, ready to eat, but Haley's chair was still empty.

I started to lift my slice toward my mouth when Mom said, "Honey, wait."

"Laurie, it's going to get cold," Dad said.

"This is a family vacation. Is it so hard for us to all sit down and eat as a family?" Mom put her napkin back on the table and went upstairs to get Haley.

Dad twiddled his fingers like he had a plan. He stood up quickly. "Mom said we have to eat dinner as a family, but she didn't say anything about having snacks as a family." He raised his eyebrow. "What do you think?" He opened up the cupboard where we kept all the junk food. "An appetizer course of cheese curls?"

I nodded. My silly dad.

"We need to eat them fast, though." Dad poured a bunch into my open hands.

"No problem!"

We gobbled them up and were still licking our orange fingers when Mom came down with Haley.

Haley's hair was dripping wet and she had already

changed into her pajamas. "Why are you licking your fingers?" she asked me, laughing. "You are so weird sometimes."

I shrugged and looked at Dad. "I guess I am."

"So weird," Dad said, reaching for a slice of pizza.

"I'd like to propose a toast." Mom raised her glass. "To one whole day of Haley and Quinnen getting along like they used to."

Dad raised his glass, too. "Amen to that!"

Haley rolled her eyes and raised her glass of root beer. "To ridiculous parents!"

"To pizza!" I said, clinking my glass with Haley's.

We all knocked glasses with each other and followed up with gulps of root beer. Haley picked off her pepperoni slices and ate them one by one. Mom and Dad brainstormed ideas for things to do the next day.

When all the pizza was gone, Haley and I cleared the table while Mom and Dad went into the living room to play cards.

"You want to watch a movie tonight?" Haley asked.

"Sure," I said, dumping some bits of crust into the trash can. "Which one?"

"I don't care. You can pick."

"Really?" Haley never let me pick the movie unless Mom and Dad made her.

"Yeah," she said. She had been washing the silverware, but she stopped for a moment to look out the window. "Unless . . ."

"What?"

"Never mind. Mom probably wouldn't let us." She went back to washing the dishes.

"Come on. You know I hate when you start saying something and then don't tell me what you were going to say."

"Fine. But I know they'll veto it," she said. "Going for a swim. At night."

"That's the best idea ever, Hales!"

I ran into the living room. "Mom, Dad—can me and Haley go swimming?"

"Right now?" Dad asked.

Mom looked up from her laptop. She wasn't supposed to bring it on vacation. "It's pitch-black out there."

Dad peered out the window overlooking the lake. "Laurie, it's a full moon."

"Oh," Mom said. I'm sure she was trying to think of some other reason why we shouldn't do it. *Sharks?*

"It's their vacation, too," Dad continued. Then he turned to me and said, "I'm fine with it if your mother agrees."

I put on my most-responsible-person-ever face. Then I wiped the pizza sauce off the side of my mouth. "Please, Mom."

She sighed. "Fine. However, if you come out covered in leeches . . ." But she was smiling as she said it.

"Thank you, thank you, thank you!" I ran upstairs

to change into my bathing suit. I peeked in Haley's room. Her phone was right where I'd left it. I thought about grabbing it and checking to see if Zack had written anything back, but then I heard Haley coming up the stairs.

Please don't check.

Haley met me in the hallway in her bikini.

We grabbed towels from Mom and Dad's room and went downstairs. I shivered when we stepped out the back door. The stones marking the path down to the dock were cool under my feet. "Have you ever gone skinny-dipping before?" I asked Haley.

"I don't know." Her eyes twinkled in the moonlight. "Have I?"

I didn't ask again; I knew she meant yes.

When we came out from under the trees and walked onto the dock, the whole lake was lit by the moon. The sky was filled with thousands and thousands of stars, and the water was calm and quiet. There were no motorboats or people on Jet Skis or even a kayak. It was just me and Haley, sitting on the edge of the dock, dipping our toes in the water.

"You really should paint your toenails," she said, lightly splashing her feet in the water.

I shook my head. "No way."

"I could paint them for you tomorrow."

Even though there were lots of things Haley and I did together, she had never offered to do that. Toenail painting was a Haley and Mom thing. Dad and I were officially not invited.

"Okay. But if I don't like it, I can take it off, right?"

"You'll probably like it," she said. "I'm pretty talented."

We got real quiet then, and I thought about the phone upstairs. Was there a way to delete a text message? Were there take-backs? What if I called Zack and said it was a mistake and I was sorry and please, please, please don't tell my sister?

Haley shivered. "It's now or never," she said, standing up. She looked up at the moon, put her hands together, and dove into the water. One of those clean dives with no splashes. She popped her head up a few yards away from the dock. "It's amazing, Quinnen. Come on—jump!"

I looked up at a star and wished. Wished for that message to disappear from Haley's phone and for everything to stay just like it was right now.

And then I grabbed my nose and jumped.

I'm not sure Haley and I would have ever left the water if Mom hadn't come out and stood on the dock, bribing us with hot chocolate.

We sat in the plastic chairs on the patio behind the house, all four of us sipping our drinks and watching for shooting stars. It was Dad's idea. He had an eye for them. That or he was a really good liar. He would always jump up and point, saying he had seen one. But then none of us could ever say that we saw it, too.

"Oh, wow!" Haley shouted. "I saw one!"

Dad squinted up at the sky. "Really?"

"It was incredible."

I stared up at the sky. There was too much of it. How was I ever going to be looking at the right spot at the right time to see one?

"I'll be back in a sec," Haley said, and she went inside.

Mom and Dad and I continued to stare up at the sky, hoping we could be as lucky as Haley.

"Mom!" Haley yelled from inside the house. It was different from any yell I'd heard from her before, and I'd heard a lot of them.

Mom stood up to go inside, but before she got to the house, Haley was slamming open the sliding glass door. Her cell phone was in her hand, and there were tears streaming down her cheeks. I opened my mouth to say something, but no words came out.

Haley stared right into my eyes. "I hate you."

"Haley," Mom said. "What's wrong?"

"You couldn't let me have this one good thing, could you? You had to go and take it away."

One good thing? Did my sister really think Zack was the "one good thing" in her life?

"Just the other week, you didn't even know if he

liked you back, and now all of a sudden you decide you love him?"

Haley glared at me. The whites of her eyes stood out in the dark, reminding me of the dog we had found hurt on the side of the road last fall. Wet and whimpering and scared all at once.

"Quinnen?" Mom said. "What's going on? Will someone say something?"

"It was a mistake." I couldn't look at Mom, and I really couldn't look at Haley. All I could do was stare down at my lap.

"She texted Zack," Haley said. "She texted him and told him I wanted to break up with him."

"Quinnen!" Mom said sharply. But I still didn't look up.

"I'm sorry," I said. But I wasn't sorry. Not completely. My voice started to waver. "What if I tell him it was me?"

"It doesn't work like that," Haley said. "It's too late. He never really loved me. He wrote back 'Okay.'" She could barely get out the last word before she started crying these big gulpy sobs.

Okay.

Okay, like he was agreeing. He was okay with breaking up with my sister. Haley and Zack were over.

It had worked.

Mom wrapped Haley in her arms and the two of them walked out to the dock, leaving me and Dad alone on the patio. Dad shifted in his seat a little, like he was trying to find the words he was supposed to say to me, the words I didn't need to hear because I knew what he was going to say already. That I was the bad sister. That I shouldn't have done it.

"Your sister's very upset," Dad finally said.

I couldn't look at him, so I stared at the moon instead. "I know." I wrapped my towel around tighter, but I couldn't stop shivering.

"You really texted him?"

I nodded silently.

"What did you write?"

" 'I think we should break up.' "

Dad sighed. Mom and Haley were sitting on the edge of the dock. Mom was rubbing Haley's back, so I knew she was still crying. "Who breaks up by text message?"

"I guess everyone," I said.

He shook his head.

"One time, Casey's brother had his friend do it for him."

"That's pretty bad," Dad said with a little laugh. "Quinnen, you know this isn't funny, right?"

I nodded.

"Even if you really don't like Zack, it's not okay for you to make decisions for your sister. I know it's hard to understand—and it's hard for your mom and me, too. Haley's a teenager. There are always going to be boys. Your sister—she's social. She's going to be out there making new friends and meeting people. That's who she is. And it's changing every minute."

He cleared his throat. "There are lots of times when Mom and I think it would be so much easier if we could make decisions for you and Haley. But it doesn't work like that."

"Really?"

"Your mom and I would love to protect you and Haley from everything, honey. But it's impossible. You wouldn't want to be the one kid in your school in padding and a helmet, right?"

"Definitely not."

"Well, that means your mom and I are taking a gamble. Every day, we let you and Haley out into the world. It means mistakes happen. We all make mistakes. Lord knows I've made plenty."

Me too, I thought.

I'd wanted Haley and Zack to break up, but I didn't think it would look like this. Feel like this. The way Haley looked at me—my own sister staring right back at me with so much hate in her eyes.

I looked up at the sky, hoping for a shooting star. I needed one. Just one.

"Do you think Haley will ever forgive me?"

Dad didn't answer right away. Mom and Haley were walking back from the dock. Haley was still sniffling, but at least she had stopped sobbing.

"I think your sister's hurting right now, and she has every right to. But it won't last forever."

"I'm sorry, Daddy."

"I know, Quinnbear. But there's someone else who needs to hear that more than me right now."

I stared at all those little gritty bits of chocolate at the bottom of my mug while Mom and Haley walked past us and into the house.

As Dad and I sat out back, watching the stars and getting colder by the minute, I saw a shooting star. A real one. I wished for a time machine, for a do-over. And then I closed my eyes real hard and counted to ten.

But when I opened them, nothing had changed. It was still just me and Dad and my mistake.

Eventually Mom came out onto the porch and told me I was going to catch a cold from sitting out there in my wet bathing suit. I didn't tell her I deserved one. I think she knew.

When I went inside, Haley was lying on the couch with a cup of tea and a box of tissues and watching *When Harry Met Sally*.

"Haley?"

I said it loud enough for her to hear, I was sure of it, but she didn't even turn her head. It was like I didn't exist.

Mom put her hand on my shoulder. "Not now, Quinnen."

I went upstairs and took a bath. When I came out, Mom was reading a book in the leather chair in my room. "We need to talk about this," she said, closing her book.

I sat down on the bottom bunk, twisting strands of wet hair between my fingers. "Okay."

"I'm so disappointed in you, Quinnen."

I nodded.

"You know better than to do something like this."

I nodded again.

"Did you read your sister's other messages with Zack?" She looked me right in the eye when she asked the question.

Looking right back at her, I told her, "No." But my lip quivered and my stupid cow eyes gave it away, like they always do.

"Oh, Quinnen."

I couldn't look at her. All I could do was picture the phone on Haley's bureau and that mean message she wrote about me to Zack. The one I was never supposed to see.

That feeling I had, that feeling that told me, *Do it now, Quinnen, do it now*, where did it go? It had worked. My plan had really worked. My sister and Zack had broken up. I had her back.

But I didn't.

Because now everything else was broken, too.

"What your sister and Zack wrote to each other was private," Mom said. "You didn't have any right to go in there and read that."

"I know, Mom," I said. "I messed up."

"Yes, you did." She was quiet for a moment. I wondered if she and Dad had talked over my punishment while I was taking a bath. *The tournament.* My eyes filled with tears.

"Not you, too," she said. "Stop that, Quinnen."

I wiped at my eyes. "Are you and Dad . . . Are you . . . Do I still get to play in the tournament?"

"Of course you do," she said. "I'm not going to punish your team. As far as we're concerned, you're going. You didn't break our trust today. You broke your sister's."

I nodded.

"You're too young to understand what it's like to have your heart broken. It's a terrible feeling. I don't know what came over you to do that to your sister."

I looked down at my lap. Mom was right. And now there was no way I could undo what I had done.

"Your father and I will discuss a punishment for you when we get home. It doesn't make sense to further spoil our family vacation." Mom sighed and shook her head. "Oh, Quinnen. You're so impulsive. Sometimes, I don't know what we're going to do with you."

She walked out of the room, leaving me all alone. I climbed into the top bunk to lie down.

It was so quiet without Haley.

Was that how it had been for her, back before I was born?

It was hard to wrap my mind around the idea of a time when I didn't exist. The thought made me shiver. But for the first six years of Haley's life, I wasn't around. There was no Quinnen. It was Mom and Dad and Haley. Just three. And then—*bam*—I was born, and suddenly it was four. Haley had to deal with me. Whether she wanted to or not. Maybe it was *not*.

Haley had never said she hated me before. She'd gotten mad at me plenty of times, so many that I had lost track. But she had never said that word. *Hate.* Did she ever wish things could go back to the way they'd been before me, when it was just three?

I could hear Dad laughing downstairs. He made fun of that movie every time Mom and Haley watched it. I bet it was him and Mom and Haley on the couch. Just three again.

I closed my eyes, rubbed the sheet in between my fingers, and tried to fall asleep.

17

{this summer}

I look back at Mom and Dad sitting in the stands, but they have no idea that Cheese Pizza is Zack. Banjo is lining up the pizzas in the foul territory over by third base. I'm standing to the side of home plate with Charlie, the old man, and Amanda, the teenager, waiting for Pizza Knockout instructions.

Banjo's voice is broadcast over the sound system. "The way the game works," he says as he heads toward us, "is each player gets paired with a pizza. Players, your goal is to knock out your pizza with . . . wait for it . . ." He looks out at the crowd, expecting them to shout out guesses. Meanwhile, the batboy and batgirl come running toward us with buckets.

"Water balloons!" Banjo yells.

The crowd cheers as the buckets are placed at our feet. We each get one bucket full of water balloons. There must be at least twenty of them in there. Red, blue, green, and yellow.

"Whoever is the first to hit their pizza ten times will win free tickets for the rest of the season and a free post-game pizza today at Pizza Palace. How about that?"

The crowd cheers again. Charlie starts reaching down for a water balloon, but Banjo cuts him off. "Not just yet, my friend. You haven't chosen your pizza partners! What'll it be, Charlie?" Banjo holds out the mic for Charlie to answer into it.

"My favorite's always been pepperoni," Charlie says.

"So pepperoni it is!" Banjo directs Charlie so he's lined up with the pepperoni pizza.

Banjo walks over to Amanda next. "Whatcha hankering for today, Amanda?"

Not cheese. Not cheese.

"I'm a vegetarian," Amanda says. "So I'll go with cheese."

"Man, my pizza craving is through the roof right now." Banjo walks over to me. "Well, sweetie, looks like you don't get much of a choice now, do you?"

"I'll take sausage," I say. But I keep looking at the cheese pizza.

"Okay, folks. We're ready to roll! On the count of three, our first-ever game of Pizza Knockout will begin!"

Banjo doesn't say that the pizzas are going to dance. He doesn't say that they're going to play the stupid "Hokey Pokey" song during Pizza Knockout. But they are. The pizzas are dancing. And they're probably happy that the day they have to wear pizza costumes is that one cool day you have all summer, where it's cloudy and it looks like it's going to rain, only it hasn't yet. And I know that underneath that costume, Zack is smiling. I can see it in the way his feet step from side to side, in the way his huge pizza body dips and twists.

Zack is happy and smiling and dancing, but my sister will never dance or smile again.

I lower my hand so it's just an inch away from touching the water balloon at the top.

"One."

Maybe this is what I've really been practicing for with Hector.

"Two."

I know I should throw at my assigned pizza.

"Three."

I grab a red water balloon, keep my eye on Zack, and throw. The balloon gets him right where his stomach should be. *Nice shot, Quinnen.* I grab a yellow balloon and watch as it explodes right by his heart.

"Hey, that's my pizza!" Amanda says. But she hasn't hit him even once.

"Oops."

I grab three more water balloons and throw them at

him. *Bam. Bam. Bam.* I can't stop. He's getting soaked, but he hasn't fallen over. Not yet.

I haven't won. Not yet.

"She's going rogue," Banjo says into the microphone with an uneasy chuckle. Putting the mic aside, he says to me, "You're supposed to be aiming for the sausage pizza."

"I guess my aim's not that good," I say.

The sausage pizza starts scooting over toward Zack, as if that will make me start hitting him, like I'm supposed to.

Pizzas are stupid.

I grab three more water balloons and chuck them even harder, this time right at Zack's head. They explode over his stupid sheer pizza eyes. I can't see Zack's real eyes, but I can feel him looking right at me, and I think he knows.

He knows that he ruined my last summer with my sister and he can never, never, never fix it.

I look down at my bucket. It's almost empty, and he's still standing. He's still standing, and the game is "knockout," and I'm going to win. For Haley.

Amanda's bucket is still half-full because she's slow and has no aim. I grab her bucket from her.

"Hey!" she says, but I don't stop. I run full speed toward Zack, clasping the bucket against my chest.

Banjo tries to run after me, but he doesn't get there fast enough. I slam into Zack with my bucket. The hard plastic digs into my chest as Zack topples over backward, and I fall to the ground. I roll off him and stand up, both arms raised up into the air, like a champion.

"Knockout!" I say.

But now that I'm close, I can see through the mesh, and when I look down at Zack, he isn't smiling. He isn't angry, either.

He's crying.

My eyes glaze over as I take in what's right before me. A teenage boy lying on the grass, surrounded by busted water balloons.

Everything I just did—it doesn't bring Haley back. It doesn't bring her back at all. And nothing will.

"Go, Bandits!" It's the only sound out of the whole crowd, and it comes from that weirdo who sits in the bleachers at every game, wearing the crazy hat with three pinwheels attached to the top and the rally monkey around his neck, the guy who yells "Go, Bandits!" at the opposing team half the time.

"I think we'll go with the regular old Pizza Race next time," Banjo says into the microphone. Some people in the crowd try to laugh with him. He hands pizza gift cards to Amanda and Charlie, who both look like they can't wait to get off the field and back into the stands.

The Coal Miners run out from their dugout and take their places for the bottom of the inning. A lady from the medical staff runs over to check on Zack, but he shrugs her off, says he's fine.

She looks down at me, sitting on the grass. "Don't you think you owe somebody an apology?"

"He ruined my life," I say. "All I did was knock him over."

She shakes her head. "Honey, that boy did no such thing."

As she walks away, I see someone running toward us from the Bandits dugout. It's Hector. But he jogs right past me. He doesn't even stop to look at me. He squats down next to Zack and talks to him. I can't hear what Zack is saying—it's muffled by the pizza costume. Hector gives him a pat on the back and stands up.

He comes over to me. "Why did you hurt my friend?"

"Your *friend*?" I look toward Zack. He's standing up and making his way back to the concession stands.

"Zack."

I take a step back. "You're friends with Zack?"

"We play music together. He lets me use his keyboard. We're thinking of starting a band, with José."

He says something else. I know he says something else, but I can't listen to it. I put my hands over my ears like I'm still a little kid and if I can't hear it, then it isn't true. With his strong hands, Hector pulls my hands off my ears. He looks confused.

"What's wrong?" he asks.

"How can you be friends with Zack?"

I look at him through blurred eyes. Now he's doing the fish thing. He opens his mouth but nothing comes out. I rub at my eyes, wipe the tears away. He doesn't know. I have to tell him.

"He took Haley away from me. My sister. She'd still be here right now if it wasn't for him."

I wait for that look to spread across his face. That moment of recognition when it all clicks into place, when he realizes his friend Zack isn't a good guy.

But I don't see it.

"No," he says. Maybe he doesn't believe me. He shakes his head and says it again. "No, Quinnen."

"Yes," I say. "Yes, yes, yes. I thought you were my friend."

"Quinnen." This time he says my name louder. Almost like Mom and Dad when they're mad.

I can't look at him anymore, and turn away. So what if Hector has to go out and pitch? He wants someone out there who's rooting for him, who's his friend? He's got him. Zack. Zack knows Spanish. He can yell *mofongo* at him. He can probably pronounce it better than me, too.

Hector doesn't need me. He never needed me anyway.

"Quinnen." Mom's sharp voice cuts through everything.

She and Dad are walking out onto the field.

Mom grabs my arm and pulls me up, like I'm a toddler. "I don't know what on earth has gotten into you, Quinnen. Attacking that young man in the pizza costume? You have a lot of explaining to do." We start walking off the field.

"It was Zack," I spit out.

Mom exchanges a look with Dad and then guides me through the gate.

We don't head back to our seats. Without another word, we pass by the booth that sells the Bandits sweatshirts and Mrs. Harrington at the ticket booth. The wind is picking up now, and the sky is dark blue all the way to the ground.

The storm is in the distance, but it feels like it's already here.

We head out into the parking lot. We walk past trucks with Bandits stickers and minivans with stickers that say "Baby on Board" and fancy cars with fancy college stickers for all the schools that Haley was supposed to visit this summer, where Haley was supposed to go next fall.

I wish she had never gotten that job at the camp. Never met Zack. Maybe then it would all be different.

Everything was fine when it was just me and Haley. But then she tried to add Zack to the equation, and it messed everything up. Zack ruined the numbers. He ruined everything.

We're in the parking lot when there's a big clap of thunder and the sky opens up. Fat raindrops splatter in the dirt. Mom holds her hands over her head as we race to the truck, but it's not enough. My T-shirt is soaked through by the time Dad is fumbling with the key.

Mom's lips are still squeezed shut like she's been holding in all the things she can't say to me in public and the second we're in the truck they're going to come flying out.

I hop into the cab through Dad's side.

"Let's talk about it when we get home, Laurie," Dad says.

And then he ruffles my hair like he always used to. "Come on, kiddo. Let's go home."

18

{last summer}

"You wanna go to the Bandits game with us?" Casey asked when I picked up the phone the morning after we got back from the Adirondacks.

"Of course."

"How about Haley?"

"No," I said. I didn't tell him that Haley hadn't spoken a word to me since the night she and Zack broke up. Even though it rained for two days straight and we were all stuck in the house. Not even during the thirteen-hour car ride home. Every time I tried to talk to her—to apologize—all she did was ignore me.

"More food money for us!" Casey said. "See you in half an hour."

I was rooting around for my Bandits shirt when the

doorbell rang. Nobody ever used the doorbell except people selling stuff or asking for donations. I went to the window to see who it was. Standing on the doorstep was Zack with a bouquet of sunflowers. Haley's favorite. Mom and Dad were in town picking up groceries, so it was just me and Haley at home.

"Haley!" I shouted.

No answer.

The doorbell rang again.

I ran downstairs and opened the door. "What are you doing here?" I asked.

"I miss her," Zack said. "Is she around?"

I nodded and let him inside. Maybe I wasn't supposed to let in strangers and Zack still felt like a stranger, but I needed to make things better with Haley. Maybe this could be the start.

I ran back upstairs, knocked on Haley's door, and waited. Nothing. "Come on, Haley. It's important."

Still nothing. I turned the doorknob; she hadn't locked it. She was lying on her bed, listening to music with her headphones on. She pulled them off the second she saw me.

"Zack's here," I said. That got her up. "He's downstairs," I whispered. "He brought flowers."

She ran over to the mirror, rubbed her face a bit, and adjusted her T-shirt.

"You look fine," I said to her.

She went downstairs. I could hear her and Zack

talking in the kitchen. She sounded like nothing was the matter, like the breakup was no big deal. I grabbed my glove and ball from off my bureau and went outside. I knew what Mom would say: Haley deserved privacy.

I ran out into the backyard and threw some killer pop-ups. It was so sunny I had to squint to see the ball. There wasn't a single cloud in the sky. I'd have to make sure to bring my cap for the game. I threw the ball higher and higher, and every time, I caught it.

Maybe things would be okay now, I thought. If Haley and Zack got back together, Haley would forgive me. She'd have to, right?

It was almost time for Casey's mom to come pick me up, so I went inside to get my Bandits cap. The sunflowers were in a vase on the kitchen counter, but Haley and Zack were nowhere in sight. I ran upstairs. That's when I heard them. They were in Haley's room.

They must have heard me coming up the stairs because Haley opened the door right as I was walking down the hallway.

"Zack and I are going to drive into Chicago and go to Millennium Park," Haley said. "They're putting on a free concert." Her whole face looked so different than it had the past few days. It wasn't just that she was smiling. Even though she and Zack had broken up, she still smiled sometimes. It was her eyes. They sparkled.

"Cool," I said. She was talking to me. She could have

left a note for Mom and Dad, or called them. But she was talking to me instead.

"You okay hanging out here until Mom and Dad get back?"

"I'm going to the Bandits game with Casey. He and his mom will be here any second."

"Fun," Zack said. "I've always wanted to go to a Bandits game. We should all go sometime. Like a double date. Casey's a guy, right?"

Haley cracked up while I pretended to vomit. "Casey is *not* my boyfriend."

"Okay," Zack said. "Just putting it out there."

Haley tugged on the sleeve of Zack's hoodie. "Let's go," she said.

I grabbed my hat and followed them outside to wait for Mrs. Sanders.

I sat down on the front porch steps with my glove. Haley and Zack got into Zack's car, but they didn't leave right away. Zack was busy saying something to Haley. He rolled down the car window. "You want us to wait with you?"

I shook my head. "I'm fine. Really." I smiled and waved.

"Okay." He gave me the thumbs-up sign, backed the car out of the driveway, and drove away.

Haley must have called Mom and Dad to ask their permission, but just in case, I scribbled down a note about where both of us were and left it on the kitchen counter under the sunflowers. When I finished, Mrs. Sanders was pulling her van into our driveway. "Who's ready to see the Bandits kick some Flyers butt?" she asked as I got into the backseat with Casey.

"Mom," Casey said. "It's not cool when you say it."

"Well, excuse me." Mrs. Sanders smiled at me in the rearview mirror. "Alert the media. I am not cool."

I smiled. The whole car ride, I thought about double-dating with Haley and Zack. I didn't think Casey understood why I had to look out the window to keep from giggling.

The Bandits were down, 4–2, in the bottom of the eighth with two outs and a runner on second when the third baseman, Ryan Gregory, stepped up to the plate and, at that moment, Mrs. Sanders's cell phone rang.

"Come on, Bandits. You've got this!" I shouted.

"All we need is a home run to tie it up," Casey said. "This is our guy."

"I know. But he's in a slump. He hasn't hit a homer in two weeks." I clasped my hands together like I was praying. "Come on, Ryan! You can do it."

Someone closer to the field level started chanting, "Let's go, Bandits," and then we were all saying it. Louder and louder.

Mrs. Sanders had her phone pressed hard to one

ear and her finger to the other ear. She was biting her lip and looking out at the game, but not like she was watching.

Ryan swung at the first pitch, and the ball smacked into the catcher's mitt.

"Strike one!" the umpire yelled.

Mrs. Sanders put her phone down on her lap. "I'm so sorry, but we need to go now."

"But the tying run's at the plate!" Casey was super-whiny when he said it, the kind of whiny Mom and Dad never let me and Haley get away with.

"I'm sorry," Mrs. Sanders said again. She put her hand on my shoulder. "We need to get you home."

The whole walk back to the car, Casey yammered on and on about how his mom had promised we could go out for ice cream after the game and how it wasn't fair that we weren't going. All I could think of was that I was in trouble. Mom and Dad must not have seen my note and didn't know where I was, and they'd had to call Haley, and Haley told them I was at the game.

I should've waited for them to get home before I left. They said I could still go to my baseball tour-nament, but they hadn't said anything about Bandits games. Maybe my punishment was going to be no Bandits games for a week, but then I went.

When Mrs. Sanders pulled into my driveway, Casey was still complaining about the broken ice-cream promise. I told them both good-bye, and Mrs. Sanders said something to me that didn't make any sense: "We love you, sweetie."

I went in through the front door.

"Mom?"

The house was so quiet I could hear the sprinkler outside. *Chk-chk-chk-chk.*

I walked into the kitchen. The sunflowers were still there. My note was still tucked under the vase. "Mom? Dad?"

Through the window, I saw the backs of their heads on the porch swing. *You're in for it now, QD.* I went out the back door, ready for my punishment.

Dad started talking first. "Hey, honey," he said, and then he took a shaky breath, the kind dads don't take. I realized I didn't have my glove. I must have left it in the van. My hand felt empty and wrong. "Your . . . your sister and Zack were in an accident on their way into the city."

I clenched my hand into a fist and stared back at Dad. "Are they okay?"

Dad slowly shook his head from side to side.

"Is she in the hospital? Can I go see her?"

But Dad kept shaking his head.

"Haley . . . died," Mom said. There was this little warble in her voice, like she had swallowed wrong. "Another car on the highway lost control, and it hit her side of the car." I kept looking at her. "They said it happened so fast she didn't feel anything."

If Haley died, they would be crying. I would be crying. And I wasn't. They weren't.

I looked at Dad and then at Mom and then at Dad again. This time, I saw the tissue folded in Dad's hand. The corner of Mom's eye that kept twitching. The salt crusties on Dad's cheeks.

No.

"I think I left my glove in Mrs. Sanders's van."

"Quinnbear," Dad said, reaching his arms out toward me.

This time he was crying.

19

{this summer}

Mom and Dad don't say anything about what happened on the field at the Bandits game. Not one word.
Dad turns on the radio to the Cubs game, and the
whole drive home, over the *swish-swish-swish* of the
windshield wipers, we listen to the play-by-play.

When we get home, I go right up to my room and
close the door. I pull out my calendar. I count five
games to figure out when Hector is pitching next.
With my fattest black marker, I cross out that game.
That whole day. I'm not going.

One, two, three, four, five. I scribble out that day,
too, so hard it bleeds onto the next month. I flip the
calendar over to August. One, two, three, four, five.
And then I'm on August 8th.

I can't scribble out that day. I can't even touch it.

I'm still looking at August 8th when Dad knocks on my door.

"Yeah?" I say.

"Can I come in?"

"Okay." I flip the calendar back to July and turn around. It's not just Dad, though. It's Mom, too. They come in and sit down on my bed.

"Honey," Mom says. "I think we need to have a talk."

"There's nothing to talk about."

Dad puts his hands on his knees and leans toward me. "Can we try?"

I nod.

He looks at Mom like they're trying to decide what to say next. The teams are all messed up now. When it was Team Mom and Dad versus Team Haley and Quinnen, at least I had a shot.

"Have you talked to Zack? Since the funeral?" I ask. Zack had come with his grandmother. There were about a million people dressed in black and navy blue telling me how sorry they were and hugging me. But real me had floated away like a little balloon. Real me was far away, watching robot me say "Thank you" over and over and over again.

Mom nods. "I've run into him around town here and there. And of course we said hi to him when we saw him at the pizza stand."

"You knew he was working at the stadium?"

"Not before today," Dad says. "Actually, we were

pretty surprised to see him there. You must have seen him there before, huh?"

"How does he get to— Why did he get a job there?"

"I don't know, Quinnbear," Dad says.

I rub my sneaker against the edge of my desk. "Did you know he's friends with Hector, too?"

"No, sweetie," Mom says.

"It's like he's trying to take everything that's mine," I say, staring at the Bandits sticker on my headboard.

"I doubt that's his goal, Quinnen," Dad says.

"Well, it sure feels like it!" I don't intend to shout it, but that's how it comes out.

Mom looks startled. "Quinnen," she says softly.

"First he takes Haley away from me, and then he starts working at the pizza stand so I can't even get my snacks and Casey has to do it for me, and then he's friends with Hector, my only real friend since Haley died. All I have left is Casey! And now he's on vacation, so really I have nobody. Don't you get it? I. Have. Nobody."

"You don't have nobody," Dad says. "You know you have us."

"Your dad's right," Mom says. "You always have us."

"No, I don't. It's not the same."

"What do you mean?" Mom asks.

"I don't want to play tennis or be in a book club or whatever thing you wished you could do with Haley. I'm not Haley. I can't be Haley."

Mom cringes. "Nobody's expecting that, honey."

Dad takes a deep breath. "This past year has been hard for all of us. We all miss her. We're all fumbling. And we're trying—we really are trying to help you, even if it doesn't always feel that way." He looks up at my Bandits poster for a second. "That's why we got . . . Anyway, Quinnbear, what can we do? How can we help you?"

"I don't know!" I close my eyes when I say it. When I open them up again, the tears are there. It's still me and my parents. Just the three of us. It'll never be four again.

"I want to take it back. All of it. All of last summer. I want a do-over." I think about Zack's face, when I finally saw it behind the pizza costume, and how he was crying. And the nail polish, Haley's favorite color. "It wasn't Zack's fault. It was me. My fault. I'm the one who ruined everything."

"Quinnen," Dad says.

"No!" I shout again. "All last summer, I never told Haley what was really bothering me. I never told her how I missed her, or that it hurt my feelings when she ditched me and how she always wanted to hang out with her friends and Zack instead of me. And then it was too late. It was too late, and I messed it all up."

I stare down at my lap, at my stupid hands that are way too big for my glove. I don't deserve to play baseball, to be good at it again.

"I never got to tell her I was sorry."

"Quinnen, honey," Mom says. There are tears pooling in her eyes.

I don't think she's ever going to stop crying, and that's my fault, too. I made my mom cry. I can't do anything right.

Mom reaches out her hand and takes hold of mine. "Haley knew—she always knew that you loved her."

"I miss her," I say. "I miss her so much I can't even believe it."

"I know," Mom says. "I miss her, too. Every day."

"Then why can't we talk about her more? I don't like pretending she was never here. I can't keep doing it."

"You know, you're right, Quinnen," Dad says.

The chair makes a creak when I stand up and squish myself onto the bed between the two of them.

It's three now. Just three. But three's a lot better than one.

I'm hugging them, and they're both hugging me, and then Mom is rubbing my back. She keeps saying the thing I've wanted to hear for so long, the thing nobody told me after Haley died. "It's okay, sweetie. It's okay."

Even though it's not, I still need to hear it.

20

{last summer}

"Are you sure, sweetie?" Dad asked. My right hand was on the door handle, my left hand inside my glove. It was two days after the funeral, and Dad had driven me all the way to Indiana for the baseball tournament.

I can do this.

"Yeah. I'm fine," I said. I hopped down from the truck and walked toward the field, toward my team. Everyone was there already. For the first time I could remember, I was late.

Jordan was warming up on the mound, tossing pitches to Katie. Did Jordan think he was going to pitch instead of me?

"Quinnen?" Katie yelled. She stood up as Jordan's pitch bounced in the dirt in front of home plate. She grabbed the ball and ran to meet me by the bench. "I didn't think you were coming," she said. "I'm so sorry about Haley."

"Thank you," I said. I had said it so many times over the past week that it came out automatically.

Nobody else came over to talk to me while I put on my cleats. Jaden and Andrew were getting drinks from their water bottles. For once they didn't give me dirty looks or crack jokes under their breath, even though Coach wasn't watching. Instead, they gave me these weird fake smiles. Coach Napoli was busy talking to the other team's coach. Once my cleats were all laced up, I slid my hand into my glove and jogged to the mound.

"Hey, QD," Jordan said. "Let me know if you change your mind. I'm ready."

I nodded and stuck my hand out for the ball.

And then it was me pitching to Katie, like I had all season. Coach told us once about muscle memory, how your body has a way of remembering how to do something if you've done it enough times. My muscles remembered how to do it, how to throw the ball where I was supposed to, even though my heart and my brain didn't.

The balls whizzed out of my hand, in an arc for one pitch, in a line for the next. Every time, right into Katie's glove.

I can do this, I told myself. *I. Can. Do. This.*

The bleachers were filling up with people who had driven all the way here to watch the games that we had worked so hard for. All spring long, all summer long. Grandmas and grandpas. Moms and dads. Aunts and uncles. Those weirdos who always came to these tournaments even though they didn't know anybody on the team. Brothers.

Sisters.

It was time to let the other team take the field to warm up. I jogged back to the bench for my water bottle. My mouth was dry, but no matter how much water I drank, it was never enough.

Casey was sitting on the bench, swinging his legs back and forth as he munched on a chocolate-chip granola bar. He smiled at me, but I could tell he didn't know what to say. It wasn't like Casey to keep quiet like this.

He wasn't the only one, though. Hardly anyone said hi. It was like they weren't expecting me to show up. Like they thought I would ditch the team for our most important game yet. You never ditch your team. That was rule number one of being a Panther. Panthers always have each other's backs.

And then it was time. Game time. They considered us the home team for this game, so we took the field at the top of the inning. I walked out to the mound, scuffing my cleats in the dirt. Katie put on her catcher's mask. She was right there. Just like always.

The leadoff batter stepped up to the plate. A righty. He jiggled his bat above his head, like he was one of the pros. I gripped the ball tight in my hand, felt the stitching cutting into it, and waited.

"Yeah, Quinnen!" one of the Panthers yelled from the bench.

"Come on, Quinnen, you've got this." Mrs. Sanders.

"You can do it!" Dad.

"Let's go, QD." Coach Napoli.

I waited and waited. Waited for her voice to yell out from the rainbow-striped chair where she always sat. She occasionally missed one of my games, but she never missed an important one. She never missed a tournament. I waited, and I waited, and I waited.

And then I understood.

I wasn't going to hear her again. She was never going to pick me up after practice. She was never going to be on the other side of my bedroom wall, tapping with her knuckles after we were supposed to be asleep. She was never going to be in the backseat next to me for a long car ride. She was never going to sit next to me at the kitchen table for dinner. Her stocking wouldn't be hung next to mine by the fireplace on Christmas Eve. I was never going to have to wait for her to be done in the bathroom on a school morning. She was never going to do anything, be anywhere ever again.

My sister was gone.

I was never going to hear Haley's voice again.

And that's when I did it. The thing a pitcher is never ever, ever, ever supposed to do. I didn't wait for the coach. I didn't wait for the next batter, or the next inning, or the next anything. I walked right off the mound in the middle of the biggest tournament we had ever played in.

When Coach Napoli called out my name, I stopped. Stopped walking and started running. I ran until I was at the edge of the woods by the field and there was no one to tell me not to and I took my glove off my hand and chucked it, as far as it would go.

21

{this summer}

"We love you, Quinnen," Mom whispers as she kisses the top of my head. She stops rubbing my back, but she still has her arm around me.

"To the moon and back, kiddo." Dad squeezes my hand.

And then nobody says anything for the longest time, and we sit on the bed as the thunder roars overhead and the rain pelts the roof so hard it sounds like hail. I wonder if they've called off the Bandits game yet.

I glance over at the signed ball sitting on my bedside table. "I miss Brandon."

Dad laughs. "You? Miss Brandon?"

"What's so weird about that?" I ask, reaching for the ball. I show Mom and Dad Brandon's signature.

"He ate all our food," Mom says. "And he always left the toilet seat up."

"I wouldn't call that his greatest flaw." Dad chuckled, turning the ball over in his hand. "You been checking up on him?"

"Not since a few days ago," I say.

"What are we waiting for?" Dad says. "Let's find out what our old buddy Brandon's been up to."

Mom and I follow Dad downstairs to the kitchen, where he turns on the computer. As we wait for it to boot up, Mom pours glasses of milk and puts Oreos on a plate. I stack two Oreos together, dunk them in the milk, and cram them into my mouth. Mom carefully slides her Oreo apart and scrapes off the frosting with her teeth, exactly how Haley used to.

"Here we go." Dad pulls up the website for Brandon's Double-A team. On the main page, there's a picture of Brandon pitching. One of those funny shots that shows his face while he's in the middle of throwing a pitch. It looks like his tongue is going to poke through his cheek.

Dad scrolls down to see how the last game went. "Ouch," he says.

Mom and I read the article along with him. Brandon gave up six runs in his second start for the Double-A team. Someone on the opposing team hit a grand slam off him. *Yikes.*

"He keeps pitching like that, he'll be back in town

before long." Dad dunks his Oreo in the milk, leaving it there for so long I can't believe the cookie comes out in one piece.

"You think so?" Mom asks.

"Nah," Dad says. "I'm sure he'll get his act together."

"Can he stay here again if he doesn't?" I ask.

Dad doesn't answer right away. He glances over my head at Mom.

"What?" I ask. It drives me crazy when they do this.

"Your mom and I have been talking about this whole hosting deal," Dad says.

I bite my lip and wait for what he's going to say next. *Please, please, please let us host again.*

"My only worry is that it's hard to have someone come and stay here—be a part of the family—and then leave. Sometimes with no warning," Mom says.

Dad looks at me. "What do you think, kiddo?"

Mom's right. At least a little. But then I think about the letter Brandon left me. How I'll be able to follow him his whole career. And how one day, when he's in the big leagues—and I know he'll get there—we can all root for him. Drive into Chicago and watch him with forty thousand other people in the stands. And how even though he's gone, I can still email him. Mom and Dad have his email address. So even though he's left, he's not really gone. Not *gone* gone.

"I think we should," I say. "As long as we don't get one of the scary tattooed guys."

Mom and Dad smile.

"I think they always send those ones to Mr. McCormack," Dad says.

"It's never going to be the same as having Haley." I look right at Mom and Dad when I say her name. "But wasn't it nice, having somebody else around? We've got a pretty big house, with Haley's room and the guest room. Could we host a couple of players?"

Dad and Mom look at each other again.

And for once they don't say "We'll see."

I'm the one who opens the door to Haley's room. It's the first time all three of us have been in here together since she died.

"It's definitely bigger than the guest room," Mom says as she picks up one of Haley's old softball trophies, the kind you get just for being on the team.

"What'll we do with her stuff?" I sit down cross-legged on the bed to take it all in.

Dad goes to the bulletin board on the wall behind Haley's desk. It's covered with pictures of Haley with Gretchen and Larissa and all her friends. With notes and drawings, cutouts from magazines, ribbons from writing contests she won. "Her friends—you think they'd want something to remember Haley by?" Dad asks.

Mom nods. "Of course."

There's so much stuff in here. Her bureau drawers and the closet full of clothes. All her books. Her computer. Her cell phone. And all the little things on her bureau and her wall.

"Us, too, right?" I ask.

"Yes," Mom says. "Anything you want to hold on to, sweetie."

"Whatever's left, we can donate," Dad says.

"When can we start?" I ask.

Mom and Dad look at each other.

"It's never going to feel right," Mom says. "So why not now?"

Dad heads up to the attic to get boxes. Mom offers to start with Haley's bureau. I start with her desk. The top drawer isn't organized at all. It's full of the kinds of things you get but can't throw away, even if no one else understands why they matter. I have one of these drawers, too—okay, a few of these drawers—but I never thought Haley had one. I never thought what might be in it. Movie ticket stubs and folded-up notes with her name on the outside and buttons for all sorts of different bands.

There are so many things in this drawer that are new to me. My sister had a whole other life apart from me and Mom and Dad: the one she shared with her friends. I save this drawer for them and start looking through her bookcase.

"Hey, Quinnen?" Dad holds up Haley's prom dress

from last year. It's green and sparkly and goes all the way to the floor. She looked so beautiful that night. "Should we hold on to this for you?" He laughs.

I snort. "Yeah, right, Dad."

But as he puts it in the pile for donations, I change my mind. "Prom's not for a long time." I carefully fold the dress and place it in my box. "You never know."

Mom pulls shirts out from Haley's bureau, considering each one before placing them into a pile for the Salvation Army.

"I loved this shirt on her," she says quietly, almost like she's talking to herself. She's holding a blue-and-white-striped shirt, nothing special.

"Keep it," I say.

She shakes her head. "Someone else needs it more than I do." She places it in the donation pile.

When she isn't looking, I put the shirt in my box to give to her later. She finds one of Haley's old Bandits sweatshirts, and I put it on. It's still too big, but someday it will be the right size.

One by one, I look at Haley's books. I haven't read any of them, haven't even heard of most of the authors before. "Hey, Mom?"

She finishes folding one of Haley's shirts. "Yeah?"

"What if we had our own book club? Just you and me. We could read some of Haley's books. We could take turns choosing the book."

"I think that would be really nice," she says, reaching for the next T-shirt.

"Can we keep them all?"

"Whatever you want, Quinnbear."

I grab Haley's jewelry box from its spot on her bureau and sit down with it on the floor. The little drawer has necklaces and bracelets, but when I pop open the top, all I see are earrings. Some are long and dangly; others are small and sparkly. Little studs and hoops in so many different colors. I pull out one of the earrings and hold it up to my ear.

"Take a look." Claudia, the woman who just used the small silver gun to punch holes in my ears, hands me a mirror.

I stare into it. Is that really me? The stones sparkle under the mall's fluorescent lights. I turn my head a little to the right, and the earrings get more sparkly, if that's even possible.

"What do you think?" Mom asks. "Do you like them?"

I hand the mirror back to Claudia. "You did a really good job," I say. "They're right where they should be. Right in the middle of my earlobe."

She laughs. "Well, I should hope so. I do this for a living."

Mom lets me pick out three new pairs of earrings,

her treat. I spend forever looking at the walls and walls of earrings. It's a hard decision. I hold a pair up to my ear and look in one of the store mirrors to imagine how they might look.

I think about what Dad said, last summer, about how Haley was changing every minute. That girl staring back at me in the mirror? She's me. Quinnen Amelia Donnelly. But she's not the same person who looked back at me in the mirror this morning while I was brushing my teeth. She's different.

Dad was right. We're all changing.

I look different on the outside, especially with these fancy earrings. But on the inside, I'm the same me. Haley's little sister. That's still me.

"You can come back and get more someday," Mom says. "There're always more earrings."

I know one pair I'm getting for sure. Tiny white baseball studs.

"Can I get dangly ones?" I ask.

Mom's leaning over the glass case with the necklaces, probably looking for something to ask Dad to get her for her birthday. "Of course," she says. "But no big hoops. They could get stuck on something, and then you'd rip a hole in your ear."

"Mom!" Some things about Mom are never going to change.

I decide on a pair of tiny silver hoops and a pair of bright blue studs for my final two choices, and take them over to Mom.

"All set?" Claudia asks.

I look at myself in the mirror one more time. "Yeah," I say. "I think so."

"You know, I brought your sister here to get her ears pierced," Mom says as we leave the store.

"Really?"

"Yup. You came, too."

We pass by the frozen yogurt shop. My stomach growls, but I don't want to stop Mom from talking about Haley. "I did?"

"You were only two. I probably had you in the stroller. Nope—I definitely had you in the stroller. It was hard to find a place to park it where you couldn't reach any of the earrings. You were awful handsy back then."

"Did Haley cry?"

"Do you think Haley cried?"

I shake my head. "What earrings did Haley get put in her ears the very first time?"

"The same ones as you."

Even though school isn't starting for another three weeks, Mom insists on checking out one of the back-to-school sales. "Just for a quick minute," she says.

Mom's minutes are never quick, but I follow her into the store anyway. She skips over the kids' section and heads straight toward the juniors'. She stops in front of a mannequin wearing the tightest jeans I've ever seen, a super-frilly pink T-shirt, and a jean jacket that looks five sizes too small. "What do you think?" she asks.

"I think you forgot who you're shopping with." I swing my bag from the jewelry store back and forth. Earrings are one thing, but Mom couldn't pay me to wear jeans that tight.

"Okay, okay," she says. "But we're not done yet."

I follow her over to the underwear section. I keep looking around to make sure there aren't any Bandits nearby. Running into one of them in the undies section would be so embarrassing. "Mom!"

"You may not need embellished jeans, but it's certainly time for some real underwear." She heads straight toward where they have all the bras on tiny hangers.

"Mom," I whisper. "I don't need a bra yet."

She turns to look at me, really look at me.

"You're right," she says. "Why rush things?"

"There is one thing I need."

She puts her hand on my shoulder. "What's that?"

"I can't remember the last time I went to a store like this," Mom says when we walk into the sporting goods store. "You always insisted that Dad take you."

It never crossed my mind that Mom would want to come. "Isn't this store the best?"

I head straight for the baseball equipment. The new

metal bats are shiny and in all kinds of colors: silver, neon green, white, gold, maroon. I run my hand over them as we make our way to the gloves. So many different shades of brown and black leather. I want to sniff them all.

"Gosh, there're so many. How do you know which one is right?" Mom asks.

I pull one off the shelf and slide my hand in. "You kind of have to go with how it feels." I point out a glove that's obviously too tiny for my hand. "You don't want one that's too small. But you don't want one that's too big, either, 'cause then it could fall off. It would really stink to make a great catch and then have your glove fall off with the ball in it."

Mom nods. "Makes sense."

A dark brown glove with a red star on it catches my eye. I reach up for it and slide my hand in. My fingertips don't quite hit the end. There's still room to grow.

I put the glove up to my face and breathe in.

"You have to sniff it?" Mom asks.

"Definitely." I grab one of the bigger gloves off the shelf and hand it to Mom. "Try this one."

"I don't know. I wouldn't know how."

"If you put on gloves in the winter, you can put on a baseball glove."

She slips her hand in and flexes the glove. "It's not very soft."

"You have to break it in, Mom."

She purses her lips. "Okay, okay."

After one more sniff, I say, "I think this is the one."

While we're waiting in line for the register, I trace the stitching on my new glove. "Hey, Mom?"

"Mmm-hmm?"

"Why did you and Dad decide to do it? To host a baseball player this summer?"

"Your father and I thought . . . well, we thought having one of the Bandits around all summer might help you realize how much you missed playing baseball. You and your sister, you were never ones to do things when we pushed them. You're so alike in that way."

As Mom steps forward to pay at the register, a tiny smile spreads across my face. *They were on my team the whole time.*

While we're leaving the store, I decide to tell her: "You know my friend Hector, the pitcher?"

Mom nods.

"He's been meeting me at the park. When I went with Brandon, it was really to meet up with Hector, to work on my pitching. I need to practice a ton if I want to be on the Panthers next year. Especially since I missed this whole season."

"I know, Quinnbear," Mom says.

My feet catch on the mall floor. "You know?"

"Do you think you'd convinced me and your father that you and *Brandon* were hanging out at the park? *The* Brandon Williams?"

"Brandon told you?"

"Let's just say your father and I aren't as clueless as you think we are." Mom laughs. "Come on, let's get you and your new glove home so you can try it out."

When we're rounding the corner to walk back to the parking garage, I see Hector's friend, the short-stop, José, waiting in line at the pretzel shop with a girl, and I know what I still have to do.

It's been almost a year since Zack was last here, in Haley's room, with me and my sister. He's standing in the doorway now, but this time it's with just me.

"It's okay," I say. "Really. I'm not going to throw anything at you. Promise."

He laughs. It's a little laugh, not at all like how he used to laugh with my sister.

The window over Haley's bed is wide open, and the curtains move with the breeze. Sunlight streams in. It's not a cave anymore. The floor is covered with boxes of her belongings, divided and labeled by Mom so it won't be hard when it comes time to donate what's left over. For the past couple days, Haley's friends have been stopping by, looking in the boxes and taking things that make them think of her.

I hop over a few boxes and sit down on the bed. Zack follows me into the room, but with slow, carefully thought-out steps.

"No one took any of her DVDs," I say. The DVD shelf next to her desk stands completely full.

Zack steps around a few piles of clothes to get there and pulls out one DVD. His hand is shaking.

There's a lump in my throat that I'm not sure will ever go away unless I say something.

"Hey, Zack?" I say it quietly, but he hears. He turns his head and looks at me. He isn't crying, but his face looks like it hurts somehow, like how Hector looked after he got hit in the face by the baseball. Like the shock of Haley dying has never left.

"I'm sorry I didn't give you much of a chance last summer. I was a little quick to judge and . . . anyway, you didn't ever do anything to deserve how I treated you. I didn't get that before, but I do. I do now, and I really am sorry."

He nods his head slightly and puts the DVD back, his hand a little less shaky.

"I should've come to see you in the hospital last summer." It comes out louder than I intend, but maybe he'll understand that I really mean it.

"It's okay," he says. "You know, I thought about giving you a call or sending you a card. But I didn't know what to say."

He goes back to looking at the DVDs, one after another. Turning them over in the palm of his hand to look at the back.

"Hey, Zack?" He doesn't look up when I say it this

time. But that's okay. All that matters is that I say it. "Haley really liked you."

"I know," he says, looking right at me. "I loved her."

"She loved you back."

I stare out the window. Dad is mowing the side yard, and Mom is busy working in the garden. The cornfields are flat and dry, which means there are only a few weeks left in the baseball season.

I turn around to see what Zack is up to. He's sitting on the floor, going through a box of random stuff from Haley's desk. Her friends have already taken a lot from that one. He picks up a glow stick from Haley's last Fourth of July.

"How did you get to be friends with Hector?" I ask.

Zack grabs some photos from the box. "He and a couple of the other players came to my band's show back in June. He liked our music and asked if we could jam sometime. I lent him my spare keyboard."

"Oh."

"You know, he misses you coming to the ball games. You're like Hector's personal mascot. I mean, in a good way. The season's almost over, and then everyone will leave."

"Is Hector leaving?"

"Everyone's got to go back home when the season ends."

"Right. Why'd you decide to work at the stadium?"

"I couldn't imagine being back . . . working at the

camp . . . without her." Zack fiddles with his lip ring. "They were hiring at the stadium, and I thought it might be nice to do something different for a change."

He goes back to flipping through the contents of the box, pulling stuff out until he has a little pile on the floor. I look through a magazine on Haley's nightstand. One of the ones with all the quizzes and dating advice. I stop at the article "How *Not* to Break Up with Your Man."

"Zack?"

He looks up, and I can tell that he'd probably like for me to leave the room and stop talking to him while he goes through Haley's belongings. But this is important.

"When I sent you that message—the breakup one—why did you write back 'Okay'?"

He keeps staring at me, but it's more like he's looking through me.

"I wish I hadn't. Those days, when you were still on your trip, when I could've talked to Haley every night—I wish I could have them back, you know?"

I nod. I know exactly.

"But when I got the text, it took me by surprise so much that I didn't know what to say."

I shift toward the edge of the bed and kick my legs against the side.

"I mean, I eventually figured out it was you. Because of the typo—how you spelled *break* wrong. But at first it didn't occur to me that someone else sent it. And then once she thought that I was okay with the idea of breaking up, she thought it meant I didn't really care about her. And I did. I liked her so much. I just . . ."

"She was so mad at me. She didn't talk to me for the whole rest of vacation." I stop kicking my legs against the bed.

"When we were in the car . . ." He covers his mouth with his hand and takes a deep breath. "After the accident, it took me so long to remember that car ride. But then my memory came back."

I bite my lip. My heart beats faster as I wait for him to continue.

"She said she was so glad I came over. She hated being mad at you, Quinnen. But she didn't know what else to do. She wanted for you to come with us, instead of going to the Bandits game." He takes in another deep breath and squeezes his eyes shut. "I'm so glad you weren't in the backseat."

"I'm sorry, Zack."

"Me too," he says.

22

{this summer}

"Ow, ow, ow!" Casey shouts, after biting into a slice of pizza at Abbott Memorial Stadium before the game.

"Not again, Case," I say.

"Yeah. Again. They shouldn't give out pizza when it's still so hot you can burn the roof of your mouth. They should wait a minute."

"Or *you* could wait a minute. Like me." I blow on my slice of pepperoni pizza and then take a huge bite, chewing loudly to make my point.

We finish our pizza at one of the picnic tables and head to our seats behind home plate to watch the end of batting practice. I look toward the dugout for Hector, but I don't see him. I wonder if he thinks I'm never going to come back.

"How long do you think we'll get free pizza for?" Casey asks.

"I don't know. Why?"

"It's a pretty sweet deal. I was hoping Zack felt bad enough that he would give you free pizza for life."

"It's not like that, Case. And anyway, Zack's not really a bad guy." I picture him playing his guitar along with Hector on keyboard. Maybe they'd let me watch them play sometime. "He's actually kind of cool."

"Do you think I would look cool with a lip ring?"

I almost choke on my soda. "No."

"Come on." Casey pinches his lip with his thumb and pointer finger. "I think it looks pretty cool."

"Then you need to look in a mirror."

"Fine, fine." He munches on his crust. "Free pizza for life, though? That would be cool."

We talk about which food we'd want to have for free for the rest of our lives if we could choose (pizza wins, but ice cream is a close second) and then what one thing we would like an infinite supply of (baseball tickets, obviously), and before long batting practice is over and the players are all warmed up and the announcer is reading today's starting lineup.

"And pitching this afternoon for the Tri-City Bandits . . . Hector Padilla!"

Hector jogs out to the mound. I keep watching for him to check my spot. To see that I came back. I missed the last four games, but I came back in time for Hector's start.

"Yeah, Hector!" I yell.

"Woo-hoo!" Casey screams.

Hector throws his warm-up pitches to the catcher. He still doesn't see me.

I stare out at the mound as Hector fingers his cross and looks up to the sky. Then he throws the first pitch.

"Striiiiike one!" the umpire yells.

Hector doesn't hesitate. He winds up and throws again: a wicked fastball.

"Striiiiike two!"

"Geez," Casey says. "He's got his good stuff."

I stand up and yell, "You've got him right where you want him!"

Hector looks into the stands, sees me, and breaks into a smile. He winds up again. The catcher doesn't even have to move his glove an inch. The ball hits the mitt with a hard smack as the batter swings and misses.

"Strike three!"

The batter walks away, shaking his head. He can't argue because he knows Hector got all those pitches in there just right. Every single person in the stadium is clapping.

But nobody is clapping louder than me.

* * *

Hector hangs in there through the seventh inning, but the manager sends out a relief pitcher for the top of the eighth.

"What are you waiting for?" Casey says. "Just go talk to him."

"It's complicated."

"Why?"

I fill him in on the pact I made with Hector and how I attacked Zack when he was dressed up as a pizza.

"I can't believe you took out a pizza," Casey says. "That's so funny."

"It didn't feel that way. Trust me."

"But you and Zack are okay now, right? Forget about that other stuff. Tackling a pizza in front of an entire stadium of people is awesome."

I had kind of forgotten about how many people saw me do it. Hiding my face behind my new glove, I say, "Do you think they'll remember me?"

Casey clears his throat. "Oh, no. Something like that? It's not memorable."

So not convincing, Casey. "Right." I get up from my seat when the top of the inning is over and walk over to the Bandits dugout. I tap my fingers on the hot metal dugout roof. "Hector?"

When he doesn't pop his head out, I crawl out onto the roof and wait for him to show his face. But he doesn't. Somebody else does, though. The manager.

"Get off that thing, Quinnen! Sheesh! You're going to get yourself hurt."

I scramble off it. "Sorry."

"Hector's in the bathroom," he says. "I'll tell him you're looking for him."

I head back to my seat and get lost in the game. The Bandits are two outs away from their first shutout in a month and you can feel it in the crowd. There's a runner on first base and everyone in the stadium is on his or her feet. Fingers crossed, arms crossed, prayers said.

They all want this one for the team. But me? I want it for Hector. This was his best start since he got hit in the face. A win for Hector.

"Come on," I whisper.

I watch as the batter makes contact with the ball. Good contact. The kind of contact that could send the runner all the way to home. But the left fielder makes a great play on the line drive and cuts the ball off, then quickly throws it back in. Still one out, but runners now on first and second.

"You've got it!" I shout. "Shake it off!"

"You want to come over to my house after the game?" Casey asks.

"Maybe."

The next batter swings at the first pitch and hits a slow roller down the third-base line. He's safe, and now the bases are loaded. I swear the whole stadium groans at once, but we're still standing, because that's what you do when you're a Bandits fan.

The pitcher takes his cap off and puts it back on—like that will suddenly make his pitches land where he wants them to? *Good luck with that.*

Someone walks down our row and stands next to me, not even asking if the seat is taken. I turn my head to see who could be that rude.

I almost drop my glove when I see that it's Hector.

"Why aren't you in the dugout?" I ask.

"The manager says it's all right. Game's almost over. My job is done."

"Right."

We watch the game in silence as the pitcher works to an 0-2 count.

"I'm sorry I left during your last game," I say.

Hector shrugs. "It's no biggie."

"Yeah, it was. To me."

"You came today. You saw me pitch well. You helped me."

"You don't need my help," I say. "I looked up the score. After the storm, you came out and pitched the rest of the game. The whole thing! A complete game? That's huge."

"Even when you weren't there, I still heard it in my head. *Mofongo.* Like how you say it."

"*Mofongo,*" I say.

He repeats it back to me. It always sounds better when he says it. "When I hear '*Mofongo,*' it makes me think about my home. I left my home to make my family proud, but really, I came to America because I

213

love playing baseball. *Mofongo* is always waiting for me back home. Right now is time for baseball."

Suddenly everyone is cheering and fireworks are going off overhead. The game is over. We weren't paying attention and missed the ending. I usually hate missing the endings, but this time it doesn't bother me.

Hector asks if we'll wait for him to get his stuff from the locker room. He wants to take us both out for ice cream. Casey checks in with his mom, who's been sitting over with her friends, to make sure it's okay, but she doesn't mind.

We're halfway to Gracie's when Hector takes a left instead of a right. "You're going the wrong way," I say.

"I forgot," he says. "We have to stop for something."

He takes another turn up at the next light. *Wait a second.* I know where we're going.

I haven't been this way in a whole year, but I know this route by heart. I look at Casey, but he shakes his head. "I don't know anything," he says.

Hector pulls the car into the parking lot at the old ball fields.

I don't know what to say.

"You never told me what really happened," he says. "So I asked some people." I look back at Casey. Casey could never keep quiet about anything. But maybe that's okay. "Zack told me about your team and what happened with your sister."

"He told you?"

Hector nods. "You and Zack, you both lost the same person. You have something in common, you know?"

Hector's right.

"Zack told me you were the star on your team. He came to one of your games, right?"

I nod. "But I left them. I ditched my team. I left them when they really needed me. I blew it."

"No," he says. "You're wrong. You didn't blow it. I called your coach. Napoli? It's too late to be on the team for this season, but he says you can still come to practice. Play with your team again."

That's them out on the field. The Panthers. Katie Miller, and Jordan, and Coach Napoli. Even Jaden and Andrew. All of them. My old team.

"What do you say?" Hector asks. He's holding out a baseball. For me.

There's a lump in my throat all of a sudden, but I swallow it down. I take the ball from Hector's hand and place it in my glove.

I give it a squeeze. "Okay."

There's this feeling in my belly that's both strange and not strange. Like I felt it once before, but a long time ago.

All I know is that the feeling makes me want to move, so I lead Hector and Casey out to the field. The ground feels different under my feet and suddenly I realize what's different. I'm not wearing my cleats. I'm not even sure if they fit anymore.

And that's when it clicks—what this feeling is. It's the feeling that I always got right before I pitched in a game. Some people call it butterflies or nerves, but Haley and I, we had our own made-up word for it: the rumbles. My insides were all rumbling around with excitement and the littlest bit of fear.

It's just practice, I tell the rumbles. *You can calm down.*

Coach Napoli waves when he sees me. He doesn't have a beard anymore. The Panthers must not be as good this year.

"We've missed you, Quinnen," he says.

"I'm sorry about last season. I—"

He cuts me off. "No worries, QD. I'm not gonna lie; we've missed your arm this year. You want to toss a few pitches from the mound?"

Of course I do. I jog to the pitcher's mound. Katie is still behind home plate. The only girl on the team. For now, at least.

"Hey, QD," she says.

"Hey, KM," I say back.

The ball that Hector gave me is still in my glove. I take a deep breath, stand up straight, and grip the ball with my right hand. The rumbles quiet down.

"Yeah, Quinnen!" Casey yells from the sidelines.

"You can do it!" Hector says.

And I hear one more voice. *You've got this, Quinn-bear.* Only I hear her in my head. When I close my eyes, I can see her, sitting in that rainbow-striped folding chair on the sidelines. Her sandals off, bare feet in the grass. My sister, Haley. She's still here. In the air, in the dirt, in the grass. In my heart.

And I think she'd agree with Hector. *Now is time for baseball.*

I take another deep breath and open my eyes. I focus in on Katie—no, on KM—crouched behind home plate, her glove in position, ready to catch my pitch.

And then I throw.

The baseball flies from my fingertips. I track its path with my eyes until KM catches it in her glove.

It's a ball. A little bit high. A little bit outside.

It's not my best pitch. Not by a lot. But I'll get there.

I wind up and throw again.

glossary of baseball terms

bat leadoff: To bat first in the starting lineup or to be the first batter in an inning.

complete game: When the starting pitcher pitches the entire game.

curveball: A type of pitch that is held and thrown in a way that makes it curve as it reaches home plate.

Cy Young Award: Named after Hall of Fame pitcher Cy Young, this award is given each year to the best pitcher in each of the two major leagues, the American and the National. It's a huge honor to win the Cy Young.

ERA: Stands for *earned run average*. To calculate a pitcher's ERA, divide the number of runs scored off her pitches by the number of innings pitched, then multiply by nine. (For example, if a pitcher gives up four runs over seven innings, her ERA would be 5.14.)

fastball: The most common type of pitch, it is thrown at or near the pitcher's maximum velocity. The speed of the ball is the primary reason why it's hard to hit.

go-ahead run: The run that gives the team that is batting the lead in a game.

grand slam: A home run with the bases loaded, scoring four runs (the most you can score with one swing of the bat).

knuckleball: This type of pitch is thrown with minimal spin, causing it to move unpredictably. The ball is held with the knuckles or fingertips. It's difficult for batters to hit and for catchers to catch. It's also difficult for pitchers to throw. As a result, very few pitchers in professional baseball are knuckleballers.

line drive: A sharply hit ball that travels almost parallel to the ground (as opposed to a fly ball, which is batted high into the air).

major league baseball (MLB): The highest level of professional baseball played in the United States and Canada. There are a total of thirty major league teams, divided between the American League and the National League.

minor league baseball: All the levels of professional baseball played below the major leagues, with official links to major league teams. In the current system, in order of descending skill level: **Triple-A** (or Class AAA), **Double-A** (or Class AA), **Single-A** (includes High-A and Low-A), **Single-A Short Season,** and **Rookie.** The Tri-City Bandits, though fictional, would be considered a Low-A team.

on-deck circle: The location in foul territory where the batter who is up next waits.

Opening Day: The first game of the baseball season. For a team that opens the regular season on the road, its first home game is regarded as Opening Day by fans in that city.

paint the corners: To throw pitches at the edges of the strike zone.

pop-up: A ball that is hit very high and stays in the infield.

road trip: A series of away games. In the low minor leagues, teams still travel by bus. But major league road trips often involve flying on a private team plane.

shutout: When a team prevents its opponent from scoring any runs in a game.

signing bonus: When high school and college players are drafted by an MLB team, they're offered money as an incentive to sign with that team. Signing bonuses for players picked in the first round are often several million dollars.

slider: This type of pitch is thrown harder than a curveball but slower than a fastball. A slider moves horizontally and drops as it gets closer to home plate.

spring training: From mid-February until Opening Day, major league teams practice together and hold exhibition games at training camps in Arizona and Florida.

starter, starting pitcher: The first pitcher in the game. Any pitcher who comes in after the starter is considered a relief pitcher. In a typical rotation, a starting pitcher will pitch every fifth game. Both Brandon and Hector begin as starting pitchers for the Bandits.

starting lineup: The official list of the players who will participate in the game when it begins.

three-two (3-2) count: Also known as a *full count*, this means a batter has three balls and two strikes. One more ball and first base is hers. One more strike and she's out!

author's note

While this is a work of fiction, **homestays,** in which host families open up their homes to minor league baseball players, are real. Single-A and Double-A teams all across the country coordinate homestays in their local communities. Though first-round draft picks often earn multimillion-dollar signing bonuses, the majority of minor league players (roughly ages eighteen to twenty-three) make very small paychecks as they begin their baseball careers. By the time they reach Triple-A, players are earning enough to afford apartments.

Most of those who take advantage of homestays are recent college or high school graduates or, as in the case of Hector, are brand-new to the United States. Their host families provide food, a spare bedroom, and an immediate connection to the community, but what they receive in return is something intangible: a lifelong connection to a baseball player. Many families will host year after year, and are likely to come to all the team's home games. A few years ago, when I went to a Kane County Cougars (Single-A) game outside of Chicago, my husband and I sat behind home plate and talked to one of the host families throughout the game. Back then, the Cougars were a minor league affiliate of the Oakland Athletics, my husband's favorite team, and this family told us about all the A's players who had stayed in their house over the years, including Joe Blanton and 2005 Rookie of the Year Huston Street.

Can you imagine being able to say an MLB All-Star stayed in your house for the summer? How about considering a famous baseball player practically part of your family?

For the host family of designated hitter and catcher Victor Martinez, a five-time All-Star and current Detroit Tiger, his one summer with them was the beginning of something special. Martinez played only one season with the Single-A Short Season Mahoning Valley Scrappers before moving up in the Cleveland Indians' organization, but far away from his home country of Venezuela, he developed a real bond with his host family. More than a dozen years later, Martinez still plays professional baseball, his son, Victor Jose, tagging along with him to games and calling his father's host mom "Grandma."

Interested in learning more about hosting and how your family might get involved? Most minor league teams that offer homestays to their players have contact information on their websites. There are also college baseball summer leagues, such as the Cape Cod Baseball League (Massachusetts), which connect players with host families.

acknowledgments

Writing a book is a lot like enduring a 162-game baseball season. There are ups and downs, boring stretches with not a whole lot of action, not to mention plenty of curveballs. The truth is, there's no way you can break into the big leagues without a mountain of support behind you.

A fingers-in-my-mouth cheering whistle for my intrepid agent, Katie Grimm, who never gave up on this book. I can't imagine not having you on my (and Quinnen's) team. I'm so grateful to my editor, Kelly Delaney, for continuing to find ways to make this manuscript stronger and for making me a better writer. And for the entire team at Knopf—Kate Gartner, Artie Bennett, Jim Armstrong, Diana Varvara, and Trish Parcell—who helped turn my Word document into this beautiful book you're now holding. I feel incredibly blessed to start my writing career at an imprint that has published so many of my favorite titles.

While there's no such thing as the minor leagues for writing, I feel deeply indebted to the writing boot camp that was the two-year MFA program in writing for children and young adults at Vermont College of Fine Arts. Thank you, Rita Williams-Garcia, for being my very first reader on the first draft of this project. I cannot put into words what it meant to me to be able to have you as a sounding board as I worked my way into this story. To Louise Hawes, Mark Karlins, and everyone who was in our summer 2012 workshop: thank you for your honest, instructive feedback, and for seeing the heart of this story even before I did. Betsy Partridge, Sarah Ellis, and A. S. King: thank you for everything you have taught me (and are still teaching me) about characters and story and plot. In the solitary world of writing, feeling like you're not doing it alone is everything. I'm so grateful for, and perpetually in awe of, my fellow M.A.G.I.C. I.F.s.

In baseball, there are the pitching and hitting coaches and an unending behind-the-scenes staff that make professional athletes look good. For us writers, it's our early readers, whose feedback on first and second and—okay—twelfth drafts helps shape the final product. Deb Alt, Gwendolyn Heasley Carter, Daniel Kenis, Alison Frew-Kimball, Erica Perkins, Jen

Petro-Roy, Cynthia Surrisi, Chin Lin Wong, and Matt Zakosek—I'm so grateful for your feedback and your friendship. To Alison Weiss, thank you for your love of Quinnen and this story and everything you brought to this manuscript. To Erin Cohen, Libby Pearson, Elizabeth Entwistle, Autumn Krause, Stephanie Matushek, Bryan Barnes, Kai Barnes—thank you for rooting for me on the long path to publication.

Even though it's been a few years since I left the library world, I can't help but count my fellow librarians among my teammates: the staffs of the Homewood (Illinois) Public Library, Concord-Carlisle High School, Gleason Public Library in Carlisle, Massachusetts, and the Malden Public Library. Thank you for the innumerable ways you have supported my writing over the years. And for all the teens who taught me so much in library writing workshops, book discussion groups, and the CCHS YA Galley Group: I hear you in the back of my head as I conceive and write each book. For my fellow Best Fiction for Young Adults Committee members: reading and discussing 200+ YA books with you was such a privilege and has deeply informed my writing. Thank you for your candid feedback and support, especially Mike Fleming, Alissa Lauzon, and Patti Tjomsland.

I would never have made it this far without the support of my parents, who've read nearly everything I've ever written and loved it all (or at least pretended to).

Thanks to my mom and dad, for everything. And to my husband, Colin, who endured what had to be the most excruciating two months of living with me imaginable, thank you for providing a sane counterpoint to my writerly crazy, day in and day out. And for grinding it out through all those games at Fenway. I know you will never love the Red Sox as I do, and that's okay.

And finally, to my home team, the Red Sox. The grit and personality of your ever-evolving team is both an inspiration and a necessary distraction from the real world. I grew up with the belief that the Red Sox would never win the World Series, and when they finally did in 2004, my world broke open. What other impossibles were possible? Thank you for teaching me to believe.

about the author

Jenn Bishop is a former youth and teen services librarian. She is a graduate of the University of Chicago, where she studied English, and Vermont College of Fine Arts, where she received her MFA in writing for children and young adults. Along with her husband and cat, Jenn lives just outside of Boston, where she roots for the Red Sox. Visit her online at JennBishop.com.